SUMMER KNIGHTS

A LADY GAYLE SUMMER MYSTERY

BOOK TWO

CASSIE RUSH

Published: June 2023

Gordian Knot Publishing

Paperback ISBN: 978-1-913948-06-1

Created with Vellum

CHAPTER ONE

Lady Gayle Summer strolled into her mother's dressing room, followed by Gaspod, her late father's bloodhound.

'Gayle, please could you leave that animal outside,' complained her mother, the Dowager Countess of Bethencourt.

'He's not doing anyone any harm, Mama,' replied Lady Gayle, fondling the large hound's soft ears. 'I have a letter from Bundle—'

'I do wish you wouldn't use such ridiculous names for each other,' replied her mother with a sigh.

'Stop fussing, Mama, and I'll tell you what's in her letter,' Lady Gayle answered her mother a little tersely. 'It's good news. She's asked me to come and stay with her and Bink— I mean Lord Ridgewell, over the New Year. That means you can go to stay with your cousin Mildred in Brighton, content in the knowledge that I won't be here alone after all.'

'Who will oversee the installation of the central heating system if you're not here though? That's what I would like to know.' The dowager countess sat back as her maid applied a brush to the countess' long hair. The maid's face was serene as she began the task of the long strokes which made the older woman's hair shine.

'I'll only be away for a few days, and Fredericks and Mrs Mitchell are perfectly capable of seeing to things here in the meantime. I rather think it will make life easier if they don't have me to cater for as well. It means all the servants can go home to their families if they wish to.'

Lady Edith Summer turned to her dressing table mirror and stared at her daughter's reflection. 'That makes sense, I suppose,' she applied a lavish layer of cream to her face.

Lady Gayle raised an eyebrow at her mother, who rarely seemed to use any form of skincare, let alone face cream, and was still becoming used to being called the Dowager Countess. The title of Countess had been hers until a few weeks beforehand when she'd unexpectedly become a widow, and Lady Gayle had inherited the entire estate. Although the stringent post-war taxes had made finances tight, they were able to make some small improvements to Bethencourt Castle, which had been in the family for several generations. Albeit not exactly Lady Gayle's branch of the family. Her inheritance came about due to the Great War and the deaths of her cousins Maxwell and Rupert, who had been amongst the vast numbers of young men lost in battle. Now the castle was hers to take care of, and the installation of central heating had been one of the first things her father had planned. Although it really was very messy and inconvenient, she wanted to carry out his wishes, even down to using the plumber he'd selected. It was why she'd written to Bundle begging for a place to stay for a while during the worst of the renovations. Bundle, always a trooper, had come up trumps, and Lady Gayle had somewhere to ne, it dated back to the reign of the Plantagenet one of the reasons that her late Great Uncle Percival led his horse Plantagenet. Despite the enormous l loss that led to her being its owner, she loved this building and everyone in it. But after the recent , she knew a break would be good for her.

escape to. However, there was one minor point that Lady Gayle was less keen on. She glanced at the letter once more.

As you know, I'm absolutely bloated at the moment. Size of a whale, I tell you. Binky has moved to his father's old room; he says there's no room in this bed for him any longer. That, and he insists the baby kicks him in his sleep. All nonsense, dash it, but you know what men are like.

Baby isn't due for a few weeks yet, and I'm committed to bed rest. Lor, am I bored. Come and keep me company. We can catch up on old times, and you can tell me everything that's been going on in your life, although...

Here, the letter broke off, the ink trailing away down the page. Lady Gayle wondered if Lady Ridgewell had dropped her pen, even though she had a good idea why the letter stopped. Only a few weeks beforehand, Lady Sylvia Redmond-Smythe had come to stay and had been a victim of mistaken identity and murdered. She sat for a moment, remembering her friend and their last few hours together.

'Gayle,' said her mother.

Lady Gayle glanced over. 'I'm sorry,' she said. 'What was the question?'

'The baby, how are you going to cope?'

'I'll be fine, Mama,' she replied, dipping her head so her mother couldn't see her flushed cheeks and flustered expression.

'Well, just so long as you are. I think we've all had enough upset for one year, don't you? Now, are you taking the Bentley?' her mother said, wiping the excess cream from her face with a tissue.

'No, Mama. Mr Howden has said I can borrow his Austin for this trip. Since he's living in the village now, he told me he can easily walk or cycle to his work here.'

'Very well. Although the thought of you driving all that way alone gives me yet more things to worry about.'

'I won't be alone. Alice will be with me. I shall telephone you as soon as I arrive. I'm going to be leaving first thing in the morning, so I simply came to wish you a very happy new year. I'm sure 1923 will be our best year ever.'

'If you say so,' replied the Dowager Countess.

LADY GAYLE RUSHED DOWN the corridor to her own room, where Alice, her maid, was putting the finishing touches to the packing.

'Are you sure that this will be enough, milady?' said Alice as she pushed down the lid of the trunk they were taking.

'Well, I do hope so, Alice. Otherwise, there won't be room for us in the car.'

'I should have sent a trunk by train, milady. I still could, but then it might not arrive in time.'

'Yes, that's the danger, isn't it? Look, it's only for a couple of nights. It's just a small house party.'

'Will Lord Charles Vickery be there?' Alice's face held a trace of concern. 'Or does he remain in mourning?'

Lady Gayle sighed. Charles Vickery had been engaged to Lady Sylvia before her death. 'Yes, I understand that Viscount Vickery will be in attendance, but then so are several other gentlemen and their ladies.'

'Lord Vickery is the only one who's still unmarried, isn't he?' A faint smile hovered on Alice's lips.

'I do believe that Sir William Greenwood is yet to take wedding vows.'

'If anyone will have him,' muttered Alice.

Lady Gayle whirled around to frown at her maid. 'Alice!

How can you say such a thing? Pon
heart. I'm sure some young lady wi
soon.'

'Yes, milady.' Alice bobbed in
mind, milady, I will send the trunk
icks is waiting for it, and then perha
bed since we're leaving so early?'

'Yes, that's a good idea,' said La
there before lunch if at all possible.
last stroll before I turn in thoug
anymore. You can head to bed.'

'Very good, milady,' said Alice. S
her coat, opened the bedroom door
rang the bell for the footmen to carry

AFTER AN EARLY BREAKFAST and a la
Fredericks, the Bethencourt butler,
and Alice were finally ready to leave. C
waiting for them.

'Drive carefully, Countess Bethenc

Lady Gayle glanced at him. *Why is*
And then she saw Mr Harry Howden
Austin. Her heart gave a little skip. Eve
tacles, he was a very handsome man.
of the staff believed he was a commu
no right to be working for a noble fa
tease them about it, and in return, Fred
agent to remember his place.

She bade farewell to her butler an
housekeeper and trotted down the few
driveway fronting Bethencourt Castle.
gaze rose to take in the splendid old ho

York s
kings–
had c
persor
ancien
turmo

How can you say such a thing? Pongo is an absolute sweetheart. I'm sure some young lady will sweep him off his feet soon.'

'Yes, milady.' Alice bobbed in a curtsy. 'If you don't mind, milady, I will send the trunk down now. Mr Fredericks is waiting for it, and then perhaps we should both go to bed since we're leaving so early?'

'Yes, that's a good idea,' said Lady Gayle. 'I'd like to get there before lunch if at all possible. I'll take Gaspod for a last stroll before I turn in though. I won't need you anymore. You can head to bed.'

'Very good, milady,' said Alice. She handed Lady Gayle her coat, opened the bedroom door for her mistress and rang the bell for the footmen to carry the trunk downstairs.

After an early breakfast and a last conversation with Fredericks, the Bethencourt butler, Lady Gayle, Gaspod, and Alice were finally ready to leave. Outside, the Austin sat waiting for them.

'Drive carefully, Countess Bethencourt,' said Fredericks.

Lady Gayle glanced at him. *Why is he using my full title?* And then she saw Mr Harry Howden on the far side of the Austin. Her heart gave a little skip. Even with his thick spectacles, he was a very handsome man. She knew that some of the staff believed he was a communist and that he had no right to be working for a noble family. Harry liked to tease them about it, and in return, Fredericks liked the land agent to remember his place.

She bade farewell to her butler and Mrs Mitchell, her housekeeper and trotted down the few steps to the gravel driveway fronting Bethencourt Castle. Looking back, her gaze rose to take in the splendid old house. Built from local

York stone, it dated back to the reign of the Plantagenet kings—one of the reasons that her late Great Uncle Percival had called his horse Plantagenet. Despite the enormous personal loss that led to her being its owner, she loved this ancient building and everyone in it. But after the recent turmoil, she knew a break would be good for her.

CHAPTER TWO

It was quite a squash in the tiny Austin Seven, and despite being very grateful to Mr Howden for the loan, Lady Gayle wondered if she could run to the expense of buying her own car in the new year. Perhaps Mr Howden could advise, as he had the best grasp on the finances of the Bethencourt estate. But enough of that, she told herself. *Let's concentrate on the drive and get there in one piece.*

She waved cheerfully to the staff, and the little car trundled happily down the drive and out onto the road heading south towards Derbyshire and the town of Bakewell, where St Nesban's House was located. It was going to be a long journey, and with the assistance of her chauffeur Chadwick, Lady Gayle had prepared the car. She had little to worry about with regard to breakdowns as she had been a mechanic in the Great War and tended to think that she often understood cars better than she did people.

Gaspod had been placed in the footwell by Alice's legs. Neither looked terribly comfortable, and the eighty-mile journey would take around four to five hours. No one would be arriving in a good mood. After a while, the additional problems of driving during the winter became apparent. Although not as bad as driving on the Western Front, the thin tyres of the Austin were liable to be lethal on icy roads. Lady Gayle was glad once more to have kept her old army boots and thick socks to counteract the worst of the cold weather. She had put them on after breakfast, grateful that her mother, who didn't approve of such mannish attire, had not risen to see her off.

The little car ate up the miles valiantly, and by late morning, they reached the outskirts of Bakewell and were only a few short miles from St Nesban's House. Lady Gayle sighed and wriggled in the driver's seat. She was tired, very cold, and her shoulders were aching dreadfully. Perhaps they should have taken a train after all? But it was so very kind of Mr Howden to loan them his car. She would have felt churlish refusing, and she had promised herself that she was going to be nicer to Mr Howden.

As they drove through the park gates, Alice gasped. St Nesbans stood on a slight rise and overlooked the parkland surrounding it. Crenelations topped each wall, which was built of dark Derbyshire gritstone. Lady Gayle had been told parts of it dated back to the Norman conquest, although, like countless stately homes, there had been many additions over the decades.

Lady Gayle's shoulders had seized up during the journey, and now she grimaced with pain as she drove the last mile to the main entrance of the splendid house. With a soft smile, she recalled the jokes that Bundle had only accepted Binky's marriage proposal after she'd seen the house. Lady Gayle grinned to herself; she didn't know how true this was, but it certainly made for a good story.

As she halted the car, Snelling, the Ridgewell family

butler, and the staff were opening doors, and Binky himself came to hand her out of the car.

'Gigi, darling,' he said and kissed her on the cheek. 'How lovely to see you. Bundle would have come down herself, but she's really tired. This baby is bound to be a boy, he's making her look huge.'

'Binky,' she replied, 'it's so good to be here. But that is such a long drive. I'm exhausted. Any chance to freshen up before seeing Bundle?'

'Why, of course. Snelling will show your maid where everything is. We've put you in the blue room; it's just along from where Bundle's room is, so you girls can have plenty of time to catch up and natter. Come along.'

Lord Ridgewell led the way into his country pile, and the first thing Lady Gayle saw were the suits of medieval armour which lined the hallway. The ones at Bethencourt Castle still had pride of place, but Lady Gayle had been thinking of donating them to the Bethencourt Museum; it would be good for the museum to have new exhibits, *if* medieval knights could be thought of as new. She looked around, and as the warmth inside the building hit her, she began to shrug off her coat. Relishing the impact of the new central heating, Lady Gayle immediately began to compare St Nesbans favourably to her beloved Bethencourt Castle.

Much as she adored her castle, she really hated chilblains.

FOLLOWING SNELLING, the aged butler up the stairs, Lady Gayle relished the pockets of warmth which hit her as she passed the cast iron radiators. She smiled to herself, knowing that this was what Bethencourt Castle would be like in a few short weeks. I cannot wait, she thought, trailing her hand over the heated surface of one of the metal beasts.

Snelling creaked along the corridor; he'd been the Ridgewell's butler for as long as Lady Gayle could remember. Even when she'd stayed at St Nesban's House long before the war, Snelling had seemed old. She thought of her own butler, Fredericks, at least she didn't have to worry about retiring him in the near future.

At last, the butler halted by an oak-panelled door, his hand resting on the brass doorknob. This, she knew, was the blue room. It was normally given to close family friends, and she suspected that it was only her room this time so that she could be near Bundle. The door swung open, and Lady Gayle was surprised to see that there was a fire burning in the grate.

'The central heating has not been installed in the bedrooms so far, my lady,' said Snelling as if he had read her mind.

Alice was already in the room and unpacking clothing; she stood upright until Snelling left them alone. Lady Gayle knew that her maid would not unpack undergarments in front of a male servant. Gaspod had taken up his usual stance on the rug in front of the fire. He was panting, probably too hot, her ladyship thought, wondering not for the first time why the dog didn't seek out somewhere cooler to sit when he overheated.

She fussed the dog and then sat down by the fire and held her hands out towards it, even though they were no longer cold after her walk through the house. Habit, she surmised.

'Hot water will be here in a moment, milady,' said Alice, 'and if you can bear waiting, you'll be served lunch when you see Lady Ridgewell. She's in her boudoir.'

Lady Gayle nodded, only half-listening. 'Yes, bed rest,' she murmured. Louder, she said. 'Do you know who else has arrived?'

'Yes, milady. Lord Vickery is here. Also, Lord and Lady Hansen arrived earlier. Even before we did. There's someone else in this corridor. She's called Mrs Bishop, but Mr Snelling referred to her as a personage. I don't believe he approves of her presence.'

Lady Gayle played with Gaspod's ears as Alice continued relating details of the whereabouts of the other guests and the locations of their bedrooms.

'Dinner is formal this evening, Mr Snelling told me, with it being New Year's Eve. He said there would be fireworks later.

'Also, Lady Ridgewell has asked if you can join her as soon as you've freshened up. I am sorry, milady. I know you wanted a rest after the long drive.'

'That's fine, Alice,' said Lady Gayle, wondering what this Mrs Bishop could have done to deserve the butler's censure. 'I haven't seen Bundle for months, so I'll just splash some water on my face, and I'll go to her. Is that what I'm wearing now?' Lady Gayle turned her attention to the golden drop-waisted dress which hung on the cupboard doors. The bodice was beaded with seed pearls and cut on the bias so that one side hung lower than the other. The skirt was a chiffon handkerchief hem, which Lady Gayle knew would make her look as if she were floating. She nodded her approval.

'I thought that one for dinner, milady,' said Alice. 'This one for now.' She held up a pale blue dress in a similar cut but without the exquisite beading.

'Yes, you're right, of course. That's much more suitable for afternoon wear. I can't wait to wear the gold one though,' she said. 'Dash it, look at the time. I had best get changed and have lunch with Bundle.'

After her toilette, Alice slipped the dress over Lady Gayle's head, fastening it at the rear. Her ladyship played with the sheer sleeves. 'Thank you,' she said to her maid before taking a final look at herself in the mirror. 'I think this is quite lovely.' She gave Alice a wink and strolled from the room.

CHAPTER THREE

Despite her best efforts, Lady Gayle was unable to find Lord Charles even though Alice had assured her that he had arrived the day before.

His new valet, a man that Lady Gayle hadn't met before, was taking care of his lordship's clothing but was unable to hazard a guess as to Lord Charles' location.

'Oh, never mind,' she said airily. 'It's nothing important, but if you could tell him that I asked after him?'

'It would be my pleasure, Countess Bethencourt,' replied the valet. His bow was deep and, to Lady Gayle's mind, a little overly obsequious. Lady Gayle had a little smile to herself. She knew Charles liked people to make a fuss over him. After all, her only reason for seeking him out was to see how he was faring after the death of his fiancée. However, it was not to be, and knowing that she would see him later at dinner, Lady Gayle headed to see her hostess.

Outside Bundle's room, Lady Gayle hesitated, not knowing what kind of reception she would receive. Despite the friendliness of Bundle's letter, it was not so very long ago she had been completely ignored by all her friends at Lady Sylvia's funeral. Even getting shot herself at the same funeral made little difference, and hardly anyone came to visit her in the hospital afterwards. 'It quite puts you off people,' she whispered to herself.

Pulling her shoulders back, Lady Gayle knocked on the door and opened it at the sound of "come in".

Bundle was reclining on a chaise lounge near a warm fire—her feet were raised on a cushion, yet her poor ankles were still terribly swollen.

'Hello Bundle. How are you, old thing,' said Lady Gayle, bending down to kiss her friend.

'Gigi, how lovely to see you. I was told you were here, and I've been holding lunch so that we could take it together. What an absolutely divine dress, you lucky thing. I suppose it'll be months before I can wear anything like that, even if I'm allowed to. Don't you have to wear hideous Victorian dresses once you become a mother?'

Lady Gayle smiled at her old school friend, glad to see that there was going to be no reticence or malice here. She exhaled—letting out all her pent-up fears in one long breath.

'It's so lovely to see you, Bundle,' she said, shaking the blue dress out a little. 'If you like this old outfit, you are going to adore the dress that Alice has ready for me to wear this evening.'

'Sounds delightful,' grinned Bundle. 'Now, do come in and sit down. Don't stand on ceremony.'

Gayle edged closer to the fire and perched on the front of an armchair. Bundle grabbed a bell and rang it until a maid appeared.

'Ah, Mary, we'll have lunch now. Thank you.' The maid

nodded and disappeared as rapidly as she had materialised. Bundle pushed herself up on the chaise lounge, and Lady Gayle rose to help her but was waved away. 'I can manage,' Bundle puffed. 'It's just a bit of a chore being so heavy. I told you that Binky has moved into his father's old dressing room, didn't I?'

'You did mention it in your letter,' replied Lady Gayle.

'What an absolute blighter he is. He gets me in this condition and then leaves me alone to suffer,' Bundle moaned. 'Oh, but you haven't heard the best of it. He wants to see the baby being born.'

Lady Gayle tried to make her mouth form a smile, but the idea of a man being present at a baby's birth was unprecedented. 'What on earth does your doctor say?'

'Totally set against it, thankfully. You know Binky, the silly blighter would only faint and then where would I be? Come in!'

The maid had returned, helped by a parlour maid to bring the meal. 'I hope you don't mind drinking tea, do you?' said Bundle. 'I can call for wine if you would prefer, but it makes me so ill these days. Would you mind pouring, Gigi? There's a darling. Just a splash of milk for me. Two sugars. I need to keep my strength up.'

Lady Gayle poured the tea as instructed and passed a cup to Bundle. Lunch seemed to consist only of soup and sandwiches, and she placed a few on a plate for her hostess. Although they were beautifully cut and the bread was whisper-thin, Lady Gayle couldn't help but notice that they were cheese sandwiches. She would have preferred cucumber. But, of course, it was the middle of winter, and perhaps cucumbers had been hard to come by.

It wasn't something she would have given much thought to until she took over the running of Bethencourt and began learning about the growing seasons of many products she'd not given much consideration to before.

She popped a few sandwiches on her own plate, watching Bundle munch contentedly. Perhaps Bundle needed the cheese. She had heard of women taking against certain foods when pregnant. Perhaps that was it.

She was on the point of pouring more tea for Bundle when there was a brief knock, and the door opened. It was Binky.

'Ah, there she is. The love of my life and mother to my son,' chirped Binky. He grabbed a couple of sandwiches from the plate and stuffed them in his mouth, chomping happily as he kissed Bundle on the cheek.

'He's convinced it's a boy,' she said to Lady Gayle as she laughed and pushed him away. 'You'll have to wait. Although a boy would be wonderful. An heir to the estate.' Bundle sighed loudly and stroked her stomach. Her face glowed. Almost like one of those paintings of the Madonna, thought Lady Gayle.

'Well, I was one of three boys,' said Binky. 'So there's a jolly good chance, don'cha think?

'Anyway, that's not what I'm here for. The others want to do some shooting this afternoon. Gigi, are you up for it?'

Lady Gayle flushed, and her mouth fell open a little. 'I'd rather not,' she said, wondering how he could be so insensitive. After recent events, Lady Gayle had made the decision that she would never touch a gun ever again. She chose her words with care. 'I've rather had my fill of shooting recently,' she murmured. 'In any case, I've had a long journey, and I didn't pack the right clothes. I'm quite happy keeping Bundle company.'

'Ah yes, gotcha. Damnable fool, that's me. I'm not too keen myself. I think I did enough shooting during the war, but it keeps the chaps happy. Well, I'll see you at dinner, Gigi. Bundle, old thing, do you think you can make it downstairs this evening? Since we have guests.'

'I'll do my best, dear,' Bundle replied quietly. 'Don't forget you promised me no card games.'

Colour rose on Binky's cheeks, and he coughed. 'Of course, I haven't forgotten, old thing, but if the guests ask me for a few hands of poker, I can hardly say no, can I?'

'Perhaps you should try?' said Bundle. She drew her lips into a thin line.

Lady Gayle glanced at the couple, wondering if she was being oversensitive to the level of tension between them. She frowned momentarily. Calm down, she told herself. *You're seeing things that aren't there.*

Binky kissed his wife on the top of her head and waggled his fingers in a childlike wave at Lady Gayle before he sauntered from the room.

'You don't have to stay with me all afternoon if you do fancy taking a potshot at our pheasants,' said Bundle.

Lady Gayle shivered. She doubted she'd ever fire a gun again as long as she lived.

CHAPTER FOUR

After Binky left, Bundle seemed rather quiet, not that she'd been swinging from the lampshades before, but she had been much chattier.

'Is everything all right?' asked Lady Gayle. 'I'm happy to eat dinner up here with you if you'd prefer not to go downstairs this evening.'

'No, it's fine. I'm getting sick of these same four walls all the time. So long as I have a rest before dinner. I want to be up to see the fireworks later,' Bundle took another sip of tea. 'And anyway, I want to see the effect you have on Charles in the dress you mentioned.'

'Charles? Why on earth would you think my dress could have any impact on Charles? I was surprised that he's here though. Isn't he still in mourning for Sylvia?'

Bundle shook her head. 'I think he's decided against it. Too morbid after the war, he told Binky. He wouldn't come to a house party if he were observing mourning, would he?'

'No, that's true,' replied Lady Gayle. Strictly speaking, she should still be in mourning for her father. Black for a year and one day, then lavender or grey for another year.

The rules were so strict for women. They were less severe for men, but she understood Charles' reticence. For this short visit, she wanted to rid herself of the black clothes she should be wearing. Wandering to the window, Lady Gayle gazed out onto the lawn and rose gardens.

'That's where we're going to have the bonfire,' Bundle chattered away, oblivious to the impact her mention of Charles Vickery had had. 'Binky has arranged for the men to build the fire out there so if I *am* too tired, I can see it from my room and not get cold.'

'That's very thoughtful of him,' Lady Gayle remarked. *Did I imagine that tension between the two of them?* 'Don't most bonfires get built weeks in advance? I'm sure the one on the village green for Bonfire Night had been growing for ages.'

'Well, this is only going to be a small one, and Binky doesn't like the idea of hedgehogs nesting in there and getting burned alive. When he was a young boy, George, his older brother, kept teasing him about it and saying they'd be eating roast hedgehog for supper.'

'I see,' said Lady Gayle. She barely remembered George. She had danced with him at a debutante ball before the war. She recalled that he trod on her toes several times, and she winced with remembered pain. His shoes had marked her satin slippers, and they were unwearable afterwards. He didn't even apologise. No, she couldn't imagine George caring one jot about hedgehogs.

ONCE THEY HAD FINISHED their late lunch, Bundle's maid insisted she lay down for a little while to rest. Lady Gayle prepared to leave her, but Bundle begged her to stay.

'Talk to me,' she said. 'You could tell me about your

handsome detective. Or you can read to me if you run out of things to say.'

Lady Gayle gave her friend a quizzical look. 'He's not my detective, and how on earth do you know he's handsome?'

'By the way you're blushing,' replied Bundle with a grin.

'Well, he's not all that handsome and in any case, I don't suppose I shall see him again.' Lady Gayle stared out of the window so that her friend could not see more blushes. As soon as she'd heard the word *handsome*, it was not Inspector Coward who came to mind but someone else entirely. Sitting on the wide window seat, Lady Gayle watched the gardeners build the bonfire. Unaware they were being watched as they threw wood on the pile, they played at jousting each other with long branches and sword fights with the shorter sticks.

'Your men are having a fine time building this fire for you. It's going to be absolutely massive,' she told her friend.

'Good. I like a big fire,' said Bundle, snuggling down on her bed. 'Now come and sit by me. Tell me how you uncovered a murderer. I want to hear all about your sleuthing.'

Lady Gayle gulped and stepped away from the window seat. It was getting darker outside now, and the men had completed their work. She related the tale to Bundle about how she had eventually exposed the real killer despite the distractions of alternative suspects. As Bundle fell asleep during the telling of the tale, Lady Gayle did wonder how boring she'd made the story and whether future narrations needed to be spiced up a little. On the other hand, since most people of her acquaintance had been friendly with Lady Sylvia, perhaps she should not be telling the story at all.

. . .

She left Bundle's bedroom with the anticipation that she might lie down for a rest herself, especially after the long journey. However, finding herself wide awake, she decided to explore. She wandered along the minstrels' gallery, leaning over the balustrade to look into the hallway below. St Nesban's House ran like clockwork, much as her own home did. Snelling, the butler, was occasionally seen. He didn't walk across the hall but seemed to glide as if he were on invisible wheels.

The housekeeper made an appearance only once. With her household keys dangling from the belt around her well-rounded waist, it was easy to see her role in the household. She glided in the same manner as the butler, but with her full-length black gown, she seemed more like a galleon in full sail.

Then the hall was still—it must have been like that for a full fifteen minutes when the grandfather clock chimed the half hour. It would soon be time to gather for dinner, and Lady Gayle pushed away from the balustrade to return to her room and change. As she began to walk to her room, she heard a noise below and peeped into the hallway. A man was running up the stairs. His dark blond hair flopped over his face, and his shirt was torn. At first, Lady Gayle thought it was one of the gardeners as the man had twigs and leaves in his hair. Unable to see the man's face from her viewpoint, she watched as he dashed down the corridor leading to the west wing. Perhaps he's one of the other guests, she thought, wondering how the man had got himself into such a state.

Before she could move away, an immaculately dressed woman strolled up the stairs, smoothing her hair. The woman was glancing around. Lady Gayle wondered where she'd been, and since the woman appeared so soon after the dishevelled man, Lady Gayle half expected the woman to pull a twig out of her sharply angled bob. She giggled and immediately put her hand over her mouth to stifle the sound. The woman below looked up, but Lady Gayle took a rapid step back so she couldn't be seen. However, the woman took the branch leading to the wing where Lady Gayle's room was. That must be Lady Elizabeth Hansen, she thought. She really was as beautiful as everyone said, but why was she behaving so furtively?

Snatching a glance at her watch, she realised she didn't have much time left to change for dinner. She returned to the blue room and swapped her tea dress for the gold beaded frock that Alice had prepared for her. When she checked her reflection in the long mirror, Lady Gayle sighed and stretched like a cat. *Now, to face the music.* She made her way downstairs and opened the drawing room door.

CHAPTER FIVE

Taking a glass of champagne offered to her by a footman, Lady Gayle listened to the chatter of the other guests before making her way further into the room. Then, as they noticed her amongst them, a hush fell over the gathering.

Lady Gayle clutched her glass tighter, taking a sip of the cool liquid. Perhaps she should have kept to her mourning clothes or avoided the party altogether. She wanted to run from the scene. All eyes were upon her, and her usual self-assurance betrayed her. Taking another sip of the champagne, as much for something to do as needing the alcohol to bolster her confidence, she looked around to see if there was a single friendly face. There was not. Lord Ridgewell had yet to join his guests, and even Charles had failed to make an appearance. Not for the first time that day, Lady Gayle wondered where Lord Vickery had got to.

Behind her, the drawing room opened once more, and everyone's attention switched to the newcomer. By the universal gasp that took place, it seemed that this guest's arrival was even more confusing than her own presence had been.

'What *is* she wearing?' a dark-haired woman hissed.

'No idea. What is she even *doing* here?' replied her companion, who Lady Gayle recognised as the stunner from the stairway.

Lady Gayle placed her now warm champagne on an occasional table and twisted around to take a fresh glass from a hovering footman. As she did so, she tried to see who was being spoken about and to take in the newcomer's appearance.

A woman of middle years, richly dressed in the latest fashion, was now chatting animatedly with Binky. Lady Gayle stepped back so she could observe the lady without being seen to stare.

Although the garments worn by the lady in question were beautifully made-to-measure, judging by the comments of the two women nearby, it was questionable whether the newcomer was a lady or not. The style, however, was intended for a much younger woman. Where the flappers wore long strings of pearls which hung straight down over their androgynous bodies, this lady's pearls gaped alarmingly over a large bosom. The dark fringed skirt skimmed the tops of dimpled knees, under which lurked substantial calves; these in turn, led down to plump feet that were encased in a pair of golden duchess shoes with a crossbar fastening.

Everything was exquisite, clearly very expensive and sadly, on the wrong person.

The buzz of conversation increased once more, mostly with the speculation of the lady's identity and why she had chosen to hog the host so rudely.

'What do you think of Binky's surprise guest?' Lady Gayle quivered as the speaker's warm breath tickled her neck and ear.

She whirled around to see Viscount Charles Vickery before her. He raised his glass to her in a jocular fashion and winked. He was as handsome as ever, and her heart performed a tiny skip.

'Who is she?' said Lady Gayle as surreptitiously as she could.

'That, my dear Gigi, is Mrs Rose Bishop.'

'That doesn't mean anything to me. Should it?'

'She is the widow of Mr John Bishop. The man who was given a posthumous gong last year.'

'I didn't realise people were given knighthoods after death,' she replied, looking up at his handsome face. 'I thought at the very least you had to be alive to be knighted.' Lady Gayle nodded. She had heard of Mr John Bishop, the munitions manufacturer, although she had not heard of his demise.

'Yes, that's normally how it goes,' said Charles with a wry smile. 'One understands that the lady insisted he still received his gong. She was dreadfully disappointed that since it was a lifetime honour, she was unable to be Lady Bishop after his death.'

'Oh dear. Was she very angry?'

'My sources tell me she was *extremely* angry.'

'Your sources?' replied Lady Gayle. She raised her eyebrow very slightly. 'I didn't know you had sources, Charles. Anyone I know?'

'Well, that would be telling, wouldn't it? Would you like to meet her?'

'Perhaps later, it looks like we're going through.' Pointing with her champagne glass, Lady Gayle indicated towards the door where Snelling had made an entrance.

'Grub's up,' yelled Binky. Snelling's face remained impassive, but Lady Gayle was sure she'd seen a slight rolling of his eyes. She dipped her head and bit her lip before she laughed out loud.

SINCE IT WAS a small gathering of only ten guests, dinner took place in the family dining room rather than the formal room, which could seat forty visitors. In this cosier atmosphere, Lady Gayle had ample opportunity to study the other guests.

She was surprised to notice that the party was somewhat unbalanced, although there were not more men than ladies—which would have been dreadful from the hostess' point of view—it was simply that she and Mrs Bishop were both widows and the only available young men, were Lord Charles Vickery and Sir William Greenwood. At least it meant she could relax and that no one was expecting her to find a new husband from this offering.

Bundle sat at the foot of the table with Charles on one side of her and Lord Hansen, who went by the nickname of Piffers, on the other side. Piffers was a very serious-looking young man with dark curly hair swept back from his forehead. At the other end of the table, sitting near Binky, was the woman she'd seen on the stairs. Even close up, Lady Elizabeth Hansen was still something of a beauty, albeit a sullen-looking one, with finger-curled blonde hair.

Lady Gayle turned her gaze to the far end of the table, wondering where the lady had been before dinner and why she had been acting so furtively. As if she was aware that she was being studied, Lady Hansen returned the gaze with raised eyebrows. Lady Gayle raised her wineglass to the lady. The gesture was not returned, and with a sigh, Lady Gayle looked away to study the other guests. Across the table, Charles caught her eye, and he winked. What on earth is he up to, she wondered, noticing his lack of black armband.

'How are you, Charles?' she said. 'I didn't get a chance to ask before dinner.'

'I'm very well. Business is booming.' He took a swig of his wine and said nothing more. Lady Gayle wondered if he was still in the same business as he had been immediately after the Great War. Although now, despite being heir to his father's estate and title, Charles had always enjoyed sailing close to the wind. There had been rumours of his needing to leave Atlantic City in something of a hurry in early 1922. Perhaps one day, he'd tell her the whole story.

Lady Gayle resumed her study of the other guests. Opposite Lady Hansen was Lady Collins, and they were opposites indeed. Pamela Collins was as dark as Lizzie Hansen was fair. She, too, wore her hair in a short bob. Hers was adorned with an ostrich feather held in place by a black beaded headband, which matched the straps on her very daring backless dress.

Next to Lady Collins was Sir William Greenwood, young and blond. She had only met him once or twice before and, despite telling Alice that he was a lovely man, she did not know him at all well. Was he the man she'd seen on the stairs? It was hard to tell since Lord Collins was also fair-haired.

When a footman drew close, Lady Gayle moved slightly to allow him to place a plate before her. She switched her attention to the food and picked up her knife and fork, noticing that Mrs Bishop had hesitated for a moment before copying Lady Gayle's movements. She gave the lady a small smile, tapping the correct fork, before reaching for her wine and taking a sip.

Continuing with her meal, Lady Gayle listened to the

conversation around her. As was often the case with people who didn't really know each other, the conversation was a little stilted. She knew she should join in but was still tired after her journey and preferred to watch for now.

'Artie, please will you stop that noise.'

Lady Gayle's gaze snapped to the end of the table. Her face flushed pink, Pamela Collins was glaring at her husband.

It was certainly true that Artie Collins had an irritating sniff, and he constantly dabbed his handkerchief at his nose. Every time he did so, a lock of his blond hair hung over his left eye, and he had to push it back into place. Lady Gayle also spotted him glance at his wife with each sniff. The frequent scowls from her had not gone unnoticed, but her outburst was completely unexpected. It was frequently a topic of gossip that it was only his incredible wealth which had enabled him to marry someone as glamorous as Pamela. As Lady Gayle watched the scene between the couple, she wondered what Lady Collins got from the relationship—were the beautiful haute couture clothes enough compensation for such a husband? Maybe they had been at some point in time. Perhaps that time had passed.

Lord Collins gave his wife a faint smile, which, to Lady Gayle's surprise, she returned.

'I'm sorry, my dear,' said Lady Collins to her husband, 'please forgive me.' Then she carried on eating as if nothing had happened.

Yes, we are a very odd party, thought Lady Gayle. Very odd indeed.

CHAPTER
SIX

Lady Gayle continued to amuse herself by contemplating the other guests and their ties to each other. The gentlemen in the party she knew had all attended the same minor public school. She and Bundle had also been at school together. Ladies Hansen and Collins were included because of their husbands, which made perfect sense. However, try as hard as she might, she really could not understand where Mrs Bishop fitted in at all.

As she mused on the connections, she caught Charles' eye, and she indicated his neighbour with a quick nod and a raise of her eyebrows. Lord Vickery grinned but gave nothing away.

Infuriating man. Time for the direct approach.

'Mrs Bishop, I don't believe we've met,' Lady Gayle began.

'We haven't,' Mrs Bishop replied. She placed a forkful of potato into her mouth.

Lady Gayle allowed silence to hang for a moment, expecting Mrs Bishop to finish her mouthful and fill the gap. When it was clear nothing more was to be said, she tried again, 'May I enquire as to your connection with Lord Ridgewell and what brings you to this delightful gathering?'

Mrs Bishop laid her knife and fork on her plate, dabbing her lips delicately with the napkin. 'We're business associates,' she finally said. 'Nothing very exciting, I'm afraid.'

'Oh gosh,' said Lady Gayle. 'I hadn't realised Binky was interested in munitions.'

'He's not,' replied Mrs Bishop, 'nor am I. No doubt you realise there's little need for munitions in peacetime.'

'No, I suppose not,' said Lady Gayle. 'Are you producing something else now?'

Mrs Bishop shook her head. 'I sold the factory when my husband died,' she said, raising the napkin to touch at the corner of her eye. There were no glistening tears to wipe away, that much Lady Gayle did notice.

'Have you finished with the Spanish Inquisition, Gigi?' said Charles. 'Mrs B is a lady of means and leisure now, aren't you?'

Mrs Bishop gave him a faint smile and inclined her head. She returned her attention to her dinner and said nothing more.

Sipping from her wine glass again, Lady Gayle decided that she'd have to wait until dinner was finished, and the ladies withdrew before she could find out anything more about this surprising guest.

However, when in the drawing room, Lady Gayle tried to engage Mrs Bishop in conversation again, but it was not to be. The lady would not be drawn on any topic despite how hard Lady Gayle tried. Even asking about the type of business that Mrs Bishop and Lord Ridgewell were engaged in was met with a severe rebuke.

'I understood that it was considered vulgar to discuss money,' said Mrs Bishop with a haughty sniff.

Lady Gayle demurred and hoped that she might find out more when the gentlemen joined them.

HOWEVER, when the gentlemen left their port and cigars for the company of the ladies, all the talk was of the day's shooting. As that conversation quietened down, Binky gave in to calls for the card table to be brought out, and the gentlemen sat down to play poker.

'Don't be too long, darling,' called Bundle to her husband. 'Poor Gigi is yawning her head off after her long drive today.'

'Oh, don't mind me,' Lady Gayle replied. 'I'll probably get a second wind before midnight.'

'Gosh, I don't think I can hold out until then, and the way Binky plays, we'll probably be penniless and cast out from the house long before then. He promised me no more gambling for money,' said Bundle. 'Binky darling, can we light the bonfire now?'

'Let me just finish this hand, old thing, then we'll toddle outside.' Binky had not once taken his eyes off his cards as he called to his wife. His lips formed a thin line, and there were beads of sweat on his forehead.

Lady Gayle glanced at Bundle. She was biting her lip, her brow wrinkled, clearly very worried. Her husband was no better at hiding his feelings. Lord Ridgewell definitely did not have a poker face. The quality of his hand was etched all over his pallid features. Lord Collins was the same; he glowered at his cards as he gripped them in his right hand. He moved a couple of cards around with his left hand but then threw them on the table in disgust.

'Are you cheating again, Vickers?' he said with a snort. 'You always have the damnedest luck.'

'I don't cheat, Artie,' replied Charles Vickery, his face devoid of expression. 'I simply don't advertise everything I'm thinking about my hand of cards. I can read your hand just by looking at your face. Binky's exactly the same.'

'It seems like cheating to me,' replied Lord Collins. He pushed away from the table and stomped over to the drinks cabinet. He poured himself a large brandy and glowered at Charles Vickery's back.

'You're just a bad loser, Artie,' said Lord Hansen. 'It's that cowardly streak of yours coming to the fore again.'

Lord Collins gripped his glass tightly, his knuckles whitening. He took a step forward towards the card table and players, but Sir William placed a hand on his forearm. Artie shook off Sir William's hand, but he did not approach the table, satisfying himself by glaring at Piffers.

The game continued for a few more minutes, and Lady Gayle was rather relieved when it ended. Lord Ridgewell tossed his cards down on the green baize, a stricken look on his face, while Charles scooped the pile of chips towards him with a broad grin.

'Where did the poker chips come from?' Lady Gayle turned to Bundle in time to see her hostess's anguished expression.

'From The 43 Club, I think. They may have been a gift from Mrs Bishop. Binky did promise me that he wasn't going to gamble for large sums anymore, but I can see he's forgotten that promise.'

'I'm sure he's not gambling too much, Bundle,' said Lady Gayle. Bundle had been one of the richest girls at their school. *Surely she can't be worrying he's going to gamble her fortune away?*

Bundle pushed herself to her feet and rang the bell for her maid. 'However much it is, it's always too much. Ah, Mary, could you fetch my coat? We're going outside now.'

The maid rushed away, and soon, the room was full of maids and valets bringing outdoor garments for their respective employers.

CHAPTER SEVEN

Outside, the wind had picked up, and it was bitingly cold. Lady Gayle pulled her winter coat collar snugly around her neck and looked back to see that Bundle was well wrapped up. Although dressed in a winter coat, Lady Ridgewell had been provided with a blanket to cover her stomach and the baby. Footmen appeared holding up torches to light the bonfire. It was even more splendid than the November fifth bonfire at Bethencourt Castle. Although, as her father's death was quite recent, the party had been a much more subdued affair. Still, she smiled to herself, all the village children had enjoyed themselves with games of blind man's bluff, passing hot potatoes, and apple bobbing. In the end, she was glad the event had not been cancelled.

'Warm enough?' Charles Vickery was by her side with two glasses of champagne in his hand. He handed one to Lady Gayle and clinked his glass with hers.

'Thank you, Charles, yes, I am warm enough, although I can't wait for them to light the fire.'

As she spoke, several footmen stepped toward the mountain of wood and thrust their flaming torches into the heap. The dry twigs and branches caught at once, and the resulting combustion produced immediate warmth. Lady Gayle rubbed her arms and edged closer to the fire. She hadn't been entirely honest with Charles about being warm enough. She breathed in the pine-scented wood smoke and closed her eyes, relishing the warmth on her face.

A scream split the air. Lady Gayle's blood froze. Bundle was trying to drag the torch out of the fire, and Binky was pulling her back. Lady Gayle stepped forward to help, and then she saw it.

'Stop,' she cried. 'Stop the fire. Look, there's a foot.' She pointed to the place where Bundle was indicating.

'Oh, my word,' said Charles. He pulled at the flaming torch, removed it from the fire, and as he did this, the footmen followed suit. Binky called for water, and it was soon on hand, dowsing the flames that were still trying to take hold.

Bundle was being comforted by Lady Hansen and Lady Collins. She was sobbing, and Binky tried to soothe her, but without success. 'Ladies, I wonder, would you mind taking my wife back to the house? Find her maid and order a hot toddy for her.'

Bundle was taken away by the ladies, and Mrs Bishop followed. Only Lady Gayle stayed behind. Taking one of the torches from the ground, she held it up. From the heap of branches and other detritus in the wood stack, a man's foot stuck out. Lady Gayle tried to move a branch to release him.

'Careful Gigi, or you'll bring the lot down.'

'We have to get him out,' she said. 'He could still be alive.'

'He's not,' said Charles. 'He's cold. There's nothing we can do. Why don't you go inside with the other ladies? Keep yourself warm.'

Lady Gayle shook her head. 'This man must have been murdered. Someone has tried to hide his body and cover up their deed. We need to call the police, and we need to find out who he is.'

Binky came to stand on the other side of her. 'The gardeners are going to dismantle the stack,' he said. 'Whoever he is, we'll soon have him out.'

Lady Gayle allowed herself to be guided to a chair that one of the footmen had brought outside for her. She watched as the gardeners dismantled all their hard work of earlier in the day.

'How on earth did he get in there? That's what I'd like to know,' said Binky.

Me too, thought Lady Gayle. *I was watching the bonfire being built all afternoon. There was no time to put a body in there. No time at all. Unless.* She thought back to the dishevelled man running up the stairs before dinner. Who *was* he? She glanced around at the other guests, inspecting their faces to see who looked worried. But everyone's face was etched with concern or shock. It was hard to separate out which face looked worried for a different reason.

After about an hour of work, the gardeners reported to Binky, who came over to Lady Gayle.

'Don't you think you should go inside now, my dear? We're about to take him out the fire, and well, not to put too fine a point on it, Gigi, well he's naked.'

She stared up at him, feeling her jaw slacken. 'Is that what you're worried about?' she said. 'I'm a widow. You know I was an ambulance driver during the war. I've seen some terrible sights, as have you. I've seen a naked man before. Can't you get someone to bring sheets to lie him on? And perhaps something to cover him?'

'It's being done, Gigi. Are you sure you won't go inside?' Lord Ridgewell's face betrayed his concerns all too clearly.

'It's for the best, Gigi,' said Charles, coming over to kneel in front of her. 'It's quite a horror. You don't want nightmares.'

Lady Gayle laughed out loud. 'I saw enough horrors when I was driving ambulances to give me nightmares for the rest of my life,' she said. 'I sat with Sylvia after she was shot. Alone in the dark and damp, I stayed with her until her body could be retrieved. I don't need to be cossetted.'

'Well, don't say I didn't warn you.' Charles rose and held his hand out to pull her from the chair. He drew her arm through the crook of his elbow, and they inched towards the bonfire. Branches lay around in aimless heaps where they had been pulled away and thrust to one side. Two footmen, aided by a couple of the gardeners, lifted the man from what would have been his funeral pyre. They laid him face down on the white sheets. His well-muscled upper back was peppered with pellet wounds from a shotgun.

Lady Gayle found herself thinking that the wound was insufficient to kill him, but the wound in his lower back certainly was. Whoever had done for this poor man had taken two shots to do so—one at a distance and one at close range.

'Turn him over,' said Binky.

One of the gardeners glanced in Lady Gayle's direction. She nodded. 'I'll be fine,' she assured him.

He nodded at the man who was rolled over. Behind her, Lady Gayle heard a loud gasp.

Well, someone knows him, she thought.

. . .

She peeked around at the people behind her, resting her gaze on each face in turn.

Artie Collins was dabbing at his nose, as usual. Pongo Greenwood was downing the remnants of a bottle of whisky he must have brought from the house. Piffers Hansen was staring at the man, too, his eyes homing in on the man's groin. Binky and Charles glimpsed quickly at each other before looking away and avoiding the other's glance. That's it, thought Lady Gayle. There's something amiss here.

'I'm going back to the house,' she said. 'I want to make sure that Bundle is well.'

'Good idea,' replied Binky. 'I don't think there's anything that we can do here. Kennard, the local bobby, should be here soon.'

Lady Gayle drew her heavy coat around her slim body. She plodded back to the house, her mind racing. Whoever the man was, he was an athlete. He had not gained those muscles from office work, and his hands were not calloused, so he had not developed them from manual work as the gardeners and farm labourers in her employ did.

Who gasped? Who knows him? Hands deep in her coat pockets and her mind deep in introspection, she didn't notice the police officer bowling towards her.

'Are you quite well, miss?' he said. 'Had a bit of a shock, have you?'

He had a kindly face which was lined with concern. 'I am very well, thank you, Constable Kennard,' she said. 'I just can't understand why he was killed and how he was placed in the bonfire.'

'Don't you worry about that, miss. Leave it all to the police. We'll get to the bottom of it. There's an inspector from Scotland Yard who will be here soon. If you just go inside in the warm. I'll be in to take statements soon.'

'Yes, of course,' she murmured, her mind still wondering about who it was she'd heard gasp. She turned away from the policeman to head back towards the drawing room. 'I'll let everyone know.'

CHAPTER EIGHT

Snelling, the butler relieved Lady Gayle of her coat when she returned to St Nesban's House. 'Thank you, Snelling. I wonder, could you ask my maid to bring my shawl down, please?' she said, shivering. 'I think I shall still feel cold for a while.'

'At once, my lady,' replied Snelling. 'Perhaps a hot toddy to chase the chills away?'

'Yes, that would be marvellous. Thank you, Snelling.' Lady Gayle opened the drawing room door and slid inside.

No one raised their heads as she entered. Everyone was deep in their own thoughts, until she approached the fire and held her hands out towards it.

Mrs Bishop was the first to speak, 'Does anyone know who the young man is?' she said.

Lady Gayle looked at her for a moment, wondering when the news that it was a young man who had been killed had reached the drawing room.

'No,' she said. 'No one seems to know who he is.' She rubbed her hands together until, at a cough by her side, she noticed Alice with her shawl. Alice placed the shawl around

Lady Gayle's shoulders and waited a moment. 'Was there anything else, Alice?' Lady Gayle glanced at her maid.

'If I could have just a moment, milady,' replied Alice. 'I think there is something you might like to know.'

'What is it, Alice?' Lady Gayle whispered.

'Lady Ridgewell wanted to talk to you before you went to bed. Her maid Mary asked me to tell you.'

'Thank you, Alice. I will go and see her before I retire for the night.'

Alice bobbed a curtsy.

Lady Gayle watched her maid leave the room, wondering what the news from below stairs would tell her. She was sure that gossip would be rife as it usually was, and that Alice would let her know everything that was important.

Turning back to Mrs Bishop, Lady Gayle said, 'When did you get the news that it was a young man?'

Mrs Bishop flushed and drank quickly from her glass, 'I'm not sure who told me. I think it was the butler.'

'I see,' said Lady Gayle. 'It *was* a young man. However, no one appears to know who he was or how he got into the bonfire. It all seems very strange. I sat with Lady Ridgewell all afternoon and watched the bonfire being built. I'm sure if anyone had placed a body in there, I would have seen it.'

'One would hope so, my dear,' said Mrs Bishop. 'Here, have this hot toddy, and come and sit down.' She took the steaming glass from Snelling's tray, placed it in Lady Gayle's hands, and guided her towards the sofa.

Although surprised at the sudden change in Mrs Bishop's demeanour, Lady Gayle took a sip of the hot liquid, and her body relished the warmth. Just then, the drawing room door opened. The gentleman had returned.

Immediately, Charles Vickery was at her side. 'How are you, Gigi? Have you recovered from the shock?'

'I'm perfectly fine, Charles,' she said. 'Mrs Bishop has been taking care of me. Is there any more news about who the young man is?'

'No,' said Charles. He glanced at Mrs Bishop. 'Nobody has a clue who he is or what he was doing here.'

Lady Gayle looked at the mantelpiece as the clock began to strike midnight. It was highly unlikely that anyone would want to see fireworks now. 'Are you sure that you've never seen him before, Charles,' she said. 'I thought you and Binky—'

'No,' Charles snapped. 'None of us have seen him before.'

Lady Gayle nodded but remembered the glance that Charles and Binky had exchanged. *What was that all about?* Aloud, she said. 'I think I'll say goodnight to Bundle and turn in. I'm exhausted. Will PC Kennard want to question us this evening? Or perhaps I should say morning?'

'You go to bed,' said Charles. 'We'll take care of the policeman.'

'Then I'll head up now. Binky, I shall pop in to see Bundle. Thank you for a lovely evening.' Binky gave her a quizzical look as if he expected her to be pulling his leg, but he nodded, and as she left the room to amble up the stairs, she could not help but wonder who the man she'd seen before dinner had been.

Once upstairs, she listened for a moment at Bundle's door before knocking. The door opened a crack, and Mary peeked out. 'Lady Ridgewell is asleep now,' she said.

'Very well, tell her I asked for her, won't you?'

'Yes, milady,' Mary replied.

. . .

Lady Gayle strolled down the corridor to her room, where Alice awaited her.

'Oh, milady, what a dreadful thing to happen,' the maid began.

'It is, indeed, Alice. What news from below stairs? What's the gossip from the servants' hall?'

'We don't gossip, milady,' said Alice with the merest hint of a sniff. 'That would be ever so common, wouldn't it?'

'It would indeed, Alice,' replied Lady Gayle, giving her a smile. 'I can't understand how the man got into the bonfire. I was watching the gardeners build it all afternoon. I certainly didn't see them placing a dead body amongst the branches.'

'The gardeners stopped as soon as it got dark, didn't they, milady? Couldn't someone have put him there under cover of darkness?'

'Yes, I suppose so, but who? We were all at dinner, from half past seven. Although, I suppose that does leave several hours from four in the afternoon until we went outside at nine o'clock.'

'That's a very long time, milady. It took us less time to drive from Yorkshire.'

Lady Gayle stepped out of the golden dress as Alice spoke. She nodded her head. 'Yes, there was plenty of opportunity,' she said. 'As for the murder weapon, all the gentlemen were using shotguns this afternoon. However, they would all have had a loader with them, so it's not as if they could dash off, kill someone, and get back without the loader knowing they had disappeared.'

'Not all the gentlemen had someone to load their guns for them today. Sir William and Lord Vickery had to share someone, and Lord Collins said he could manage on his own.'

'No gossip from downstairs, at all,' said Lady Gayle with a grin. In the mirror, she saw Alice flush. 'So, we have three gentlemen who don't have a full alibi. All the gentlemen had the means, and now we simply need to find out—apart from the identity of the victim—who had a motive to kill him.'

'There was something else, milady,' said Alice. She dipped her head and regarded her mistress in the mirror's reflection through lowered lashes. 'I saw a young man leaving Mrs Bishop's room this afternoon.'

'A young man? What kind of a young man?' asked Lady Gayle. She recalled how Mrs Bishop had known the victim was a young man when she was convinced the news had not reached the drawing room. Although she would need to ask Snelling if he had divulged the information to the assembled company—just to be sure.

'Tall, well dressed, but not a gentleman. I asked the other maids, and he's not been seen here before, according to them. I did think he was rather handsome though,' said Alice with a sigh.

'I saw two people acting rather furtively this afternoon—a dishevelled blond man on the stairs. I didn't see his face, but he can't have been our victim. He was far too thin. Then I saw Lady Hansen returning to her room, but there was something about the way she was looking around. It was as if she didn't want to be spotted by anyone.'

'There are always a lot of people wandering around at a weekend house party, milady. And neither could have put the man in the bonfire, could they?'

'No, definitely not,' said Lady Gayle, 'However, I cannot

say if the young man was well dressed at all since he had no clothes on when I saw him, but I would place money on his not being a gentleman. Far too well-muscled. And his hands weren't soft. They weren't rough either, but they looked like very strong and capable hands.'

CHAPTER NINE

It wasn't yet light when Lady Gayle awoke. She threw back the covers and slid out of bed. Once at the window, she pushed the heavy curtains aside. It would be light soon, and needing a breath of fresh air, she decided to take Gaspod for a walk in the park.

She slipped into a tweed calf-length skirt, topped it with a warm jumper and popped her feet into her old army boots, once again grateful for the thick socks that she'd brought with her. 'Come on, boy,' she said. 'Let's have a nice New Year's Day walk.'

As she wandered downstairs into the great hall at St Nesban's House, she caught sight of several servants scurrying around preparing the house for the still-sleeping guests. A side door she knew led out into the garden, and she strolled towards it and slipped out into the dawn.

The lawn was cut quite short near the house, small strands of grass dotted about showed that even though it was winter, the gardeners had given it a recent trim. Despite that, the dew was abundant, and her boots were soon covered in droplets. Chadwick, her chauffeur, also undertook some indoor duties, and he had given her boots a good coating of dubbin wax before they left Bethencourt Castle, so fortunately, the moisture did not seep through to her feet. Shoving her hands into the deep coat pockets, she wandered towards the edge of the formal garden. Below in the valley, gauzy grey tendrils left a smoky trail as they exited chimneys she realised must be down in the village, but which were well out of sight. She glanced back at the windows of St Nesban's House; above stairs, all the curtains were drawn. No one stirred, but in the village down in the valley and below stairs, there would be, she knew, frantic flurries of activity.

She headed towards the steps which left the formal gardens to walk in the parkland below when she heard someone call her name. Binky waved his flat cap in greeting as he headed towards her.

'I say, old thing,' he said. 'You're up dashed early. Fancy some company?'

'That would be lovely,' she said, watching him scratch Gaspod behind the ears. They continued down the steps and into the taller meadow grass of the park. Gaspod ran ahead, his nose to the ground and his tail high.

'Terrible business that yesterday,' said Binky. He slashed at some tall grasses with his walking stick, and Lady Gayle kept quiet, waiting for him to say what it was he'd come to say.

After a while, she gave up, 'Yes, terrible, and so strange that young man turning up like that,' she said. 'Did you know him?'

Out the corner of her eye, she saw Binky give her a surreptitious glance.

'I may have done,' he said.

'Oh dear, Binky. Where did you know him from?'

Binky said nothing, and she cursed herself for asking such direct questions. A change of subject was necessary, she decided. 'How was the pheasant shooting yesterday?'

'Good,' replied Binky. His shoulders relaxed with the change in subject, and on safer ground, he talked about the birds shot and the number of braces ready for the table. 'Would you like to take a brace of pheasant back yourself when you leave?'

'That would be lovely,' she replied. 'I'm sure Mrs Woods can make her delicious game pie. I haven't had one of those for years. Not since before the war.'

'That seems an awfully long time, Gigi.'

'Yes, it is, isn't it?' Lady Gayle fell silent for a moment. Then she remembered her purpose. 'Did you shoot all afternoon? It must have been very cold.'

'Snelling and a couple of the footmen brought an early tea out to us. Soup, sandwiches, and some hot toddies. Most welcome,' said Binky.

'Were all the chaps there?' asked Lady Gayle. She stared off into the half distance as if the question were of no consequence.

'Yes, everyone was there,' said Binky. 'Look, I know what you're getting at. No one sloped off to shoot random strangers, I can assure you.'

'Was he a random stranger though, Binky? Didn't you just say you think you may have known him from just after the war?'

Binky slashed at more tall grasses, the blades gave way under the vicious onslaught and collapsed. 'No. I didn't say *when* I knew him, just that I may have. I was rather wild after I left the army,' he said. 'Did a lot of stupid things. But that was before I married Bundle and settled down. She's done me a lot of good has Bundle.' He hung his head and smacked the toes of his boots with the walking stick.

Lady Gayle allowed him a few moments of silence. She recalled her own time immediately after leaving the ambulance service. Her father was already next in line for Bethencourt Castle, her mother was delighted with the rise in social position and fortune, and she, well she was newly widowed and fed up with everything. She'd seen no future at that time and had been pretty wild herself. Drugs, gambling, drinking, wild parties—she'd tried almost everything she could think of to rid herself of the interminable grief.

'I ran up some debts,' Binky murmured so quietly she scarcely heard him.

'Many debts?' she whispered, thinking that it was no wonder that Bundle had been so upset the night before.

Binky nodded. 'The gambling got pretty out of hand. All good now, of course,' he said. 'All paid off.' He glanced at her quickly before flushing and looking away again.

Lady Gayle pretended not to notice his flush, but she did wonder why he'd been talking to Bundle about selling off the family silver. There's more to this story, she thought as she realised Binky must have run up yet more debt.

'Whoever the man was, Binky,' said Lady Gayle, 'someone killed him and covered that up by hiding his body. He came here to see someone. If that wasn't you, then it was one of your guests.'

Binky sniffed and slashed at the innocent grasses again. 'I must get back to the house,' he said suddenly. 'Bundle will be awake soon. I should see how she is. This has all been a terrible shock for her, especially in her condition. Good morning, Lady Gayle.'

Binky touched his fingertips to his flat cap and strode

back to the house. Lady Gayle stared after him, wondering about his sudden change in mood and formality. Unbidden, the idea that Binky knew a lot more about the young man's death than he was prepared to admit flooded into her mind. She shook her head, trying to rid herself of the thought. If Binky was found guilty, he would leave a widow and a fatherless child behind. Although she would not allow that to happen, it was clear that his lordship was not behaving like an innocent man.

CHAPTER TEN

Gaspod nuzzled at her skirt, and Lady Gayle patted him on his head absentmindedly. She closed her eyes briefly, recalling the scene from the night before and the man's naked corpse. Snapping her eyes open, she wondered where on earth the victim's clothes could be. To her mind, it made far more sense to destroy the clothes with the body. She crossed her arms over her chest, watching her breath hang in the cold air. As she headed towards the stables, someone called her name.

Not again, she thought. Turning around, she spotted Viscount Charles Vickery striding towards her. She fixed a smile in place despite her frustration at her search plans being cut short.

'Have you forgotten there's been a murder,' he hissed, concern etched across his handsome face. 'Do you think it wise to wander around alone? Or have you just wiped what happened last time from your memory?'

'I scarcely think I'm likely to forget, Charles,' she said, tracing the partially healed scar on her neck with her fingertips. 'I don't think I'm a target this time though, do you?'

'Hard to say,' said Charles. He held out his arm, and just like the night before, she complied, and her hand was tucked into the crook of his elbow. He patted her hand. 'That fits there rather well, don't you think?'

Lady Gayle said nothing, but she didn't remove her hand. She was familiar with Charles and his flirtations. It's just his way, she told herself. *He means nothing by it.* 'How are you?' she said.

'I'm fine. You?'

'Well, it was quite a shock to see that young man discarded so ruthlessly last night. But I was wondering about you. After all, it wasn't my fiancée who was killed recently...'

'Ah yes, my beloved Sylvia,' said Charles with a cough. 'I've decided to put on a brave face. Stiff upper lip and all that.'

Lady Gayle glanced up at him just in time to see his jutted-out jaw give way to a momentary quiver of his chin. Perhaps he's more upset than he lets on, she thought. When her husband, Hugh, died, she carried on for weeks, trying to put his death from her mind with hard work. That had been easy during the Great War. Much less so afterwards, in peacetime. Yes, she knew all about putting on a brave face.

Whilst she was still puzzled by Charles' lack of any external signs of mourning, she decided to allow him this moment of quietude. Lady Gayle sneaked another glance at Charles, who was biting his lip. There had been times in the past when she wondered how much in love with the wealthy Lady Sylvia Charles really had been, but seeing him here biting back his tears, she was overwhelmed with guilt for her lack of faith in him.

'Did you have a good shoot yesterday?' she said, using the same change of subject she'd used with Binky.

'I hope you're not asking if I added men to my bag. I stuck with pheasants, thank you very much,' he retorted.

'Did you have a decent loader with you? I heard they were in rather short supply.'

'Now I wonder where you heard that,' exclaimed Charles. He removed her hand from his elbow and turned to face her, still holding her hands in his. 'Stay out of this, Gigi, you could get hurt.'

'I only asked about the sport yesterday afternoon,' she said, in wide-eyed astonishment at his change in mood. 'Nothing more than that.'

'Well, since there were only two men available for loading, it could have been much better. Binky's gamekeeper was with him; Piffers and I shared the under-keeper. He was a competent enough fellow.'

'And were all the guns there all afternoon?'

'Now you come to mention it,' said Charles, 'I think Pongo disappeared after Snelling delivered a hot snack to us. He didn't have a loader, and when we resumed, I don't recall hearing the shots as loudly as they had been. Piffers was on my left. Binky on my right. Artie and Pongo were at the far end.'

'I think I saw someone running upstairs just before dinner,' said Lady Gayle, 'they were in a bit of a mess, twigs in their hair—'

'Now this is exactly what I'm talking about, Gigi,' Charles said. 'Don't interfere. You're not a detective, and it's not your place to find out who killed the young man. Leave it to the police.'

'Who do you think was running upstairs in a mess though,' she persisted.

'Did you see which way they went?' Charles said with a sigh.

'To the west wing where you're sleeping.'

'Could have been *either* Artie or Pongo then. More likely to be Pongo,' laughed Charles.

'Why do you say that?'

'He's having a fling with Lizzie Hansen, that's why. And so when I noticed he wasn't at the shoot any longer, I said nothing. I thought Pongo and Lizzie would be...' he broke off and winked at her. 'Well, you know.'

'What does Lord Hansen think about it? He can't be at all happy with the situation,' said Lady Gayle.

'I think as long as Piffers is left alone with his valet, he really doesn't mind what his wife gets up to at all.'

Lady Gayle frowned up at Charles for a moment. He winked suggestively, and she suddenly caught on. 'I didn't know,' she said.

'Not many people do,' said Charles. 'Best to keep that sort of thing hush-hush, don't you think? I wouldn't want to be responsible for him going to jail.' At the sound of a car on the gravel driveway, he turned.

'Who's that,' said Charles, peering at the vehicle.

'I expect it's the doctor,' replied Lady Gayle. 'Binky is rather worried about the impact this upset is having on Bundle. I expect he asked Snelling to request a visit.'

'Yes, I suppose so,' said Charles. 'Anyway, I'm rather peckish. I'm going to head in for some brekker. Are you coming?'

Lady Gayle shook her head. 'Maybe later,' she said. As she watched, a man alighted from the car. He collected a Gladstone bag from the rear seat, and Lady Gayle smiled to herself. She'd been correct in her assessment, and she decided that she, too, had better check on her hostess after the doctor had left.

Once inside the house, Lady Gayle peeked into the dining room. Only the gentlemen were there, tucking into what looked like mounds of kedgeree. Binky was not present, of course. *He must be with Bundle.* Deciding to have breakfast in her room, she made her way upstairs.

'I'll have a chat with Bundle and then see if I can speak with the ladies,' she murmured to herself.

When she arrived at the blue room, Alice had a fire and fresh footwear waiting. 'I've sent down for a good breakfast for you, milady,' Alice said.

'Good luck with that, Alice. I popped my head into the dining room, and the gentlemen were all eating kedgeree.'

Alice nodded but didn't reply. Breakfast, when it arrived, was a bowl of porridge and the anticipated dish of rice, eggs, and haddock. Lady and maid exchanged glances.

'Cook has been told to cut back on expenses,' said Alice.

Lady Gayle nodded and ate what she could. Later, she left the dog with Alice and made her way to Bundle's room. Mary, the maid, was leaving, and she held the door open for Lady Gayle. 'His lordship is still in there, but I'm sure they won't mind,' she said.

Lady Gayle thanked the woman and strolled through the doorway.

'She's asking the most damnably impertinent questions,' she heard Binky saying.

'What about dear?' Bundle replied.

'About the man who was killed. Did I know him that sort of thing? I say you don't think she's gone off her rocker since that thing in November, do you?'

'Binky darling, I don't believe any such thing, and nor

do you,' Bundle said to her husband. 'If Gigi was asking about the murdered man, then that's quite normal. I'm sure all our guests are thinking exactly the same. I'm confident if you'd strolled with any of them this morning, they would have asked the very same questions.'

'Well, if you're certain,' said Binky.

'I am,' said Bundle. 'Oh, Gigi, there you are. We were just talking about you. Were your ears burning?'

'Nothing terrible, I hope.' Lady Gayle moved further into the room, hoping that they hadn't realised she'd been eavesdropping. 'I only came to see how you were. When is the detective from Scotland Yard expected?'

'He should be here by lunchtime,' said Binky. 'I was told that they would drive through the night. The Chief Constable said there would be a couple of constables with him so they could change drivers on the way.'

CHAPTER
ELEVEN

Lady Gayle shut the door after Binky had left. She turned to Bundle, who was still in bed with a warm knitted shawl around her shoulders. 'How are you this morning?'

'Better than the young man in the woodpile,' said Bundle. 'Do we have any idea who he is yet?'

'No,' said Lady Gayle. She decided to keep the information that Alice had seen a stranger in the house to herself for the time being. 'Perhaps the detective from Scotland Yard may know who he is?'

'Yes, perhaps. Come and sit by me. How are things with you and Charles?' Bundle smiled gently at Lady Gayle through lowered lashes. 'Isn't he as handsome as ever?'

With a slight raise of her shoulders, Lady Gayle smiled at her friend, 'Yes, he's still very good-looking, and we'll always be great friends. However, I don't believe we will ever be anything more than that. He's still very upset about Lady Sylvia, even if he doesn't show it.'

'If you say so,' muttered Bundle. 'Personally, and for goodness sake, don't tell anyone I said this, but I rather think he's more upset about losing her fortune.'

. . .

'OH BUNDLE, where do you get these ideas?' said Lady Gayle briskly. 'Perhaps you're spending too much time alone up here? Have you thought about that? Are you sure that you're perfectly well after the shock yesterday? Is everything fine with the baby?'

'Gosh, what a lot of questions. Yes, Gigi, baby and I are splendid,' said Bundle, picking up Lady Gayle's hand and squeezing it. 'Obviously, I am worried. It's my first baby; that's why I wanted you here.'

'I'm not a nurse,' said Lady Gayle. 'If anything happens—if the baby starts to come, I—I won't be any use. I suppose I can still drive fast, and I could get you to the hospital, but please don't ask me to do anything more than that.' Lady Gayle rose and began to pace the room whilst biting her fingernails.

'Gigi, is there something you're not telling me? Come along, how long have we been friends? You know you can tell me anything.'

Lady Gayle stopped pacing and glanced at her friend. She exhaled deeply and bit her lip. She placed her hands protectively over her stomach but shook her head, saying, 'No, there's nothing. Nothing that you need to know.'

'Oh, Gigi, why didn't you tell me?' Bundle gasped. 'When did it happen? No, silly me, of course, it happened before Hugh died.'

Lady Gayle collapsed into an armchair by the newly laid kindling in the grate. She shivered and looked around for matches to light the fire.

'Gigi, for heaven's sake, get it alight and then tell me what's happening,' Bundle demanded.

'There's nothing to tell, really,' said Lady Gayle. 'It

happened just after Hugh died. I hardly knew I was pregnant. Anyway, it's all a long time ago now, isn't it?'

'Is losing a child ever a long time ago?' whispered Bundle.

Lady Gayle shrugged, thrusting a lit match into the pile of newspaper and sticks. She blinked away tears and scrabbled around in her pockets for a handkerchief. 'I can't think about that now,' said Lady Gayle. 'We have to focus on you and your baby.'

'And is that why you're ignoring Charles' attentions?' Bundle pushed her bed covers back and swung her legs out of bed. She pulled on a dressing gown, drawing it around her middle, covering her enormous belly. She approached Lady Gayle tentatively, holding out her hands. 'Are you afraid you can't have more babies? Or afraid that you'll lose another baby?'

'Yes,' Lady Gayle laughed harshly. 'All of the above. I'm terrified Bundle. After what happened before Christmas, I don't think that I can trust my own judgements of people. I'm terrified of falling in love again. Terrified of becoming pregnant and scared of losing another child. So, there you have it. That's me in a nutshell—one big pile of fear and mistrust. And you know what? I hate it. I hate that about me. I hate being this person. I want to go back to the woman I was in the war. Driving my ambulance, being fearless. Doing something worthwhile. I feel utterly useless now.' The tears were unstoppable; large, hot droplets ran down her face. The handkerchief was insufficient and soon became sodden.

Bundle waddled to the dressing table, where she pulled out a drawer and an embroidered sachet case. From here, she took two lace handkerchiefs. Then, thinking about it, she took two more and waddled back to her sobbing friend.

'Cry all you need to,' she said. 'I bet you haven't cried since it happened, have you?'

Lady Gayle shook her head. 'No,' she muttered, 'not really.'

'Have you told your mama?' asked Bundle, ever practical, handing her the small collection of handkerchiefs.

'Yes, she knows. I told her quite recently.'

'Other than that, you've kept it all bottled up, haven't you?' demanded Bundle, her hands on her hips. 'Oh, you're such a silly, silly girl. Come on, cry it all out.' She patted Lady Gayle on her shoulder.

Wiping her nose on the final clean handkerchief, Lady Gayle gave Bundle a weak smile. 'I can't. I think that I have done enough crying for today.'

'Promise me you won't bottle it up anymore,' said Bundle. 'I'm sure it can't do you any good.'

Lady Gayle sighed and raised her eyes to the ceiling. 'No doubt you're right,' she said, 'but we can't go against our upbringing, can we.'

Bundle laughed. Then she grimaced and lowered herself onto a chair by the fire. 'Perhaps not,' she said. 'However, sometimes I think we should.'

Lady Gayle nodded and picked up the book she'd been reading to Bundle the day before. Bundle waddled to her bed and laid down. Before too long, she was fast asleep. Lady Gayle closed the book and left.

LOOKING AT HER WATCH, she realised that it was nearing lunchtime. She quickened her step and made her way to the drawing room. When she wandered into the room, Lady Collins was alone reading a magazine.

'Good morning, Lady Collins,' said Lady Gayle. 'Did you sleep well after yesterday's disruptions?'

'Tolerably well,' came the reply. 'Call me Pamela, will you? I'm still getting used to this Lady this and Lady that nonsense.'

Lady Gayle laughed. 'I know exactly what you mean,' she said. 'I was an Honourable until a few months ago, and now I'm a Countess.'

'Yes, I heard. I am so very sorry about your papa,' said Lady Collins.

Lady Gayle dipped her head and blinked. *Dash it, I'm not going to blub again, am I?* She raised her head, 'I think I'll just get some fresh air before lunch,' she said.

Once outside the drawing room, she cursed herself for her weakness. *You're supposed to be asking questions, not bursting into tears.* She grabbed a coat from the rack in the cloakroom and exited St Nesbans by the side door, which she had used earlier that day. She paced back and forth for a moment, and once she felt she had recovered her equilibrium, she headed back to the house.

As she did so, she saw Inspector Aubrey Coward alighting from a police car and heading towards the front door of St Nesban's House.

Inspector Coward placed his trilby on his head as he stepped from the car. When he noticed Lady Gayle on the lawn, he raised his hat and strode into the house. She lifted her hand to wave in response, though when she realised his attention was no longer on her, she couldn't help but feel a little disappointed.

. . .

Lady Gayle trudged back into the house, replaced the coat in the cloakroom and was on the point of returning to her bedroom, having decided she'd embarrassed herself enough and would forgo lunch when Snelling appeared.

'Begging your pardon, my lady,' he said with his usual half bow. 'Inspector Coward would like to speak with you if it's not inconvenient.'

'Thank you, Snelling,' she said. 'Where is he?'

'He's in the library with Lord Ridgewell at the moment, my lady.'

'Thank you.' She turned towards the stairs when a thought occurred. 'Snelling, could I ask, on the night the body was found, did you tell the ladies that it was a *young* man we'd discovered in the bonfire?'

'I don't believe I mentioned his age, my lady,' replied Snelling. 'After all, how would I have known myself?'

'Just what I thought, thank you, Snelling. Look, I just want to freshen up. Could you tell the inspector I'll be along shortly?'

'Very good, my lady.'

Lady Gayle trudged up to her room. If no one had mentioned age, just how did Mrs Bishop know that it was a *young* man's body?

CHAPTER TWELVE

Lady Gayle plodded upstairs to her room. Alice was tidying away clothes, but she poured water into the wash bowl as soon as she saw her mistress' expression.

After splashing water on her face, Lady Gayle dried it. 'Inspector Coward has arrived, and he wants to see me,' she said. 'And I am such a sight.'

'I have just the thing,' said Alice. She opened the cupboard door and pulled out a heavy silk concoction with long sleeves. It was a dove grey colour and hung to the knee with a daring v-back panel of chiffon.

'That might be a bit much,' said Lady Gayle.

'Trust me,' replied Alice.

'Don't I always,' said Lady Gayle, stepping out of the tweed skirt and heavy jumper. She slipped her feet into the heels that Alice placed before her and stood while Alice fastened the double bar shoes and the dress. 'Perfect,' she said.

• • •

She left the room and edged along the corridor to the top of the stairs. Why am I so nervous, she thought. Remembering how she had left things with the inspector and not anticipating seeing him again was one concern. How she felt at seeing him again was another.

With a deep breath, she strode down the stairs towards the library. 'Inspector Coward, she cried. 'What a pleasure to see you. Happy New Year.'

'And a very Happy New Year to you too, my lady,' replied Inspector Coward. He stood by the mantelpiece and held his notebook in one hand. With it, he indicated the sofa. 'Won't you sit down, my lady?'

Lady Gayle eased herself onto the sofa and gazed up at him. *Has he lost weight? Why do you care? You are not looking for a new husband,* she reminded herself with gritted teeth.

'I am sorry that your new year has been ruined, Inspector,' she began. 'You certainly made good time getting here; you must have driven through the night.'

'Not quite my lady,' the inspector replied. 'But I was told you were here. That's why I asked to take the case.'

Lady Gayle dipped her head, hoping that he would not see her blush. 'Do you suspect me of this murder too, Inspector?' she said.

'Not this time, but you do have a terrible habit of being in the wrong place at the wrong time.'

'Perhaps it's the right place at the right time?' she countered.

'How do you make that out?'

'Well, without me, you wouldn't have an on-hand witness, Johnny on the spot or something like that.'

'I see what you mean,' replied the inspector. 'What can you tell me?'

'Sadly, very little,' she replied with a moue of disappointment. 'We all trooped out into the garden after dinner for the bonfire and fireworks, and that's when Bundle, sorry, I mean Lady Ridgewell, screamed, and we saw the foot. Then we got the poor man out of the fire. I say, you don't happen to know who he is yet, do you?'

'Yes,' said Inspector Coward. 'We have identified the victim.'

'Oh, do tell, Inspector. Is he a gangster?'

'What on earth made you ask that?' the inspector regarded her with a severe frown.

'I was simply teasing you, Inspector, but I rather thought he looked like someone who could take care of himself,' She looked at her fingernails all rough and torn from chewing them whilst talking to Bundle. She raised her head, 'My maid said he was very handsome.'

'Your maid? Does your maid know the man?'

'No, Inspector, I don't believe she knows the victim per se, but she did see someone in the house during the afternoon.'

'Why didn't she say something before now?'

'I don't know,' replied Lady Gayle. 'She wasn't to know that he was a stranger. With a house full of weekend guests, it's never easy to know who should be there and who should not.'

'Quite so. I'd like her to look at the body.'

'Of course, you do,' replied Lady Gayle. 'I'll ask her if she's prepared to do that.'

'If you wouldn't mind doing it as soon as possible,' replied Inspector Coward briskly. 'As it happens, the victim does have criminal ties. Therefore, in answer to your question, yes, I do know who he is.'

'Are you going to tell me, or is it a state secret?'

'His name is John Parsons. Most people know him as

Jack or Jackie Parsons. He was a boxer. He fought for his regiment. Was very good from what I understand, but after the war, he fell in with a bad crowd.'

'Didn't we all,' she said, thinking of her own wild times after peace had been declared. 'Which regiment was he with?'

'The Royal Fusiliers,' said Inspector Coward.

'I see,' said Lady Gayle. She wondered which regiments the chaps at the house party had been in, although she was confident that it would not be hard to find out. Again, she came back to that gasp when the body had been turned over. Someone had lied about knowing Jackie Parsons, but who? Just as she was on the point of relating this information to the inspector, one of his constables knocked on the library door and peeked into the room.

Inspector Coward nodded at the man, 'I think that will be all for now, Lady Gayle,' he said, and he held the library door open for her.

Once in the hallway, Lady Gayle was rather annoyed that her interview with Inspector Coward concluded so abruptly. She decided to have her lunch. She folded her arms and looked around at the suits of armour. What secrets did those medieval knights have, she wondered. On the point of tiptoeing across the hall to take a peek inside one—after all, it was a perfect place to hide things—Lady Gayle jumped. Snelling had silently appeared and was eying her suspiciously. With an exasperated sigh, she went to see if Bundle was awake.

'Have you had lunch yet?' Lady Ridgewell asked. 'Mary is about to collect a tray for me. You can join me if you'd like to?'

Lady Gayle nodded mutely, and Mary was dispatched to collect two trays.

'How is the Inspector?' asked Bundle. 'Is he as handsome as ever?'

Lady Gayle smiled, 'yes,' she said. 'I dare say he is. He knows the victim. A champion boxer, apparently. Boxed for his regiment.'

'Which one,'

'The Royal Fusiliers.'

'Oh, that's interesting. I wonder if Piffers knew him. He was a captain in the fusiliers.'

Lady Gayle tried not to show her interest in this snippet of information. Where had Lord Hansen been standing when Jack Parsons' face had been revealed? But he could not have disappeared when the gentlemen were shooting. Charles would have noticed since they were sharing a loader. Whilst his lordship may have known the man, he could not have killed him.

'You're very quiet,' Bundle murmured. 'Are you working out who the killer is?'

'No, of course not, Bundle,' Lady Gayle gazed out of the window towards where the bonfire had been built. 'But I do wonder what brought Mr Parsons here. Especially on New Year's Eve. It seems a strange time to make house calls.'

'Perhaps he had discovered that the person he wanted to see would be here for New Year and *only* for New Year. After all, Binky and I have no travel plans, but others do. Piffers and Lady Hansen are going to Florence as soon as they leave here. Charles returns to London; Lord Collins is going back to his Scottish estate, and Sir William is accompanying Lord and Lady Hansen.'

Lady Gayle raised her eyebrows, astonished by the arrangement. Surely Lord Hansen knows about their affair

—it's taking place under his nose, after all, she thought. Even after Charles' comments about Lord Hansen and his valet, she found it hard to believe that Piffers didn't care what his wife did. She knew such arrangements were not unknown in society, although she was quite certain it would not suit her temperament at all. Having known one loving marriage, she would not accept a bothersome arrangement. Then she laughed at herself. *Why are you even considering such things,* she thought. *You've declared to anyone who will listen that you do not want another husband.*

'Gigi, are you listening?'

Lady Gayle turned her head. 'I'm so sorry, Bundle; I was miles away.'

'Happy thoughts, I surmise, judging by the smile on your face,' said Bundle. 'My doctor has said I need to rest after meals. You can stay quietly with me, or you can go and do some sleuthing if you would prefer to.'

'I think I'll let you rest,' replied Lady Gayle. She dabbed her lips with her napkin and pushed the small table away. She looked down at the dove grey silk. She would need to change if she was going to be looking for clues.

CHAPTER THIRTEEN

After changing back into her tweed skirt and jumper, Lady Gayle took Gaspod out for another stroll in the gardens of St Nesban's House, allowing thoughts to meander randomly through her head. *What did happen to the victim's clothes? In fact, why undress him at all? It makes no sense. It's simply something else to hide, and disrobing the victim would take more time. Why not place him in the bonfire fully clothed?* The only conclusion she decided made any sense was that there must have been something special or different about the clothing. Alice had, after all, said that the man she'd seen was very well dressed. Yet, if that's the case, thought Lady Gayle, surely it makes even more sense to burn them?

Her mind racing, Lady Gayle headed to the spot where the shooting party had been on New Year's Eve. From there, she planned to trace the killer's steps to the bonfire and hoped to find the place where Mr Parsons had been shot. She gave a grim smile; it really was just like tracing the problem with an engine. Break the problem down into its component parts. Check each component, and as you discover that one works, move on to the next part. That way, little by little, piece by piece, she always worked out where the issue lay.

Ambling past the stables, Lady Gayle saw Inspector Coward's two constables, armed with pitchforks, searching each loose box. Binky's hunters were taken from their stable while the constable searched through the straw in each box. As each horse was put back into the box, the constable moved to the horse next door. It looked terribly boring, and she had a better idea.

As on her own estate, much of the acreage of St Nesbans was given to sheep farming. At this time of year, the sheep would be out on the moors, scavenging what they could from the heather and sparse grass. The shepherds often put hay out for the sheep, especially if snow was expected. In preparation for this, hay was stored in small barns on the moors. Preparation was, as she was discovering, everything in sheep farming.

Lady Gayle knew there was one sheltered barn near where the shooting party had been on New Year's Eve. *If any barn had been used to commit the murder, then surely it has to be that one.* With Gaspod scenting the ground ahead of her, Lady Gayle strode along the path. The little hut was just out of sight behind a small outcrop of the dark peak gritstone rock. *Was Mr Parsons led to his death, or had he arranged to meet someone here?*

When she reached the hut, however, she battled to push the door open. She peeked inside and allowed her eyes to become used to the low light. However, apart from the marks where she'd fought with the reluctant door, there was no sign of any disturbance. The hut appeared in perfect order. There were no cartridge cases, no scuff marks, and most irritating of all, no blood.

'Dash it all,' she muttered to herself. 'I was sure I was on the right track.'

Lady Gayle kicked at the hay which lay on the ground. There was nothing to see here, and she was frustrated and annoyed at her lack of success. Placing her hands on her hips, she gazed around inside the hut. What she really needed to find out was why. Firstly, why was Jackie Parsons here? Secondly, who wanted him dead? Those, she knew, were the types of answers which would lead to understanding why the young man had to die.

Making her way back to the house with Gaspod at her heels, she thought over the problems before her.

One: someone had left the shooting party. Two: all of them had guns. Therefore, anyone could have shot the boxer. Three: the noise from the pheasant shooting would cover up any other shotgun sounds.

She frowned and pursed her lips. Although someone definitely wanted Parsons dead, the murder wasn't planned. It was a complete contrast to the recent attempts on her own life. That killer had planned carefully. This murder had more chaos around it.

It was as if the victim was in the wrong place at the wrong time, she thought. Even the act of disposing of the body was completely random and hurried. 'Someone has something to hide, don't they, boy?' she said to Gaspod. 'Who do we know who has something to hide?'

Gaspod flopped onto his haunches and gave an ear a half-hearted scratch. Lady Gayle patted him on the head and led the way back to the house. She left the bloodhound in her room with Alice, as she knew Binky didn't like the hound loose about the house; Gaspod was no mere lapdog.

The dog had an imposing presence. When he was settled, Lady Gayle carried on with her investigations.

Once downstairs, she found Snelling. 'Where might I find Lord Hansen?' she asked.

'I believe he is in the library with Lord Ridgewell,' Snelling replied.

'Thank you,' said Lady Gayle and stepped across the hall to open the heavy wooden panelled door. Both gentlemen rose as she entered the room.

'Please sit down,' she said. 'I've just come to find something else to read to Bundle. I didn't realise there was anyone in here.'

'Piffers and I were just talking about this dreadful business,' Binky said.

'Yes, absolutely dreadful,' said Lord Hansen.

'Certainly, quite dreadful, Lord Hansen, but I understand you have a tour of Florence coming up,' said Lady Gayle. 'That will be nice to look forward to after the events here. Is it right that Sir William Greenwood is accompanying you and Lady Hansen?'

'Oh, call me Piffers,' said Piffers with an airy wave of his hand. 'Everyone does. Yes, Pongo is something of an expert on Italian art, and I was thinking of purchasing some paintings. Pongo is coming along to advise.'

'It must be lovely to have such competent friends,' said Lady Gayle. 'Someone you can completely rely on.'

'Er, yes,' said Piffers. He looked rather embarrassed, and Lady Gayle realised that he must think she was referring to her own recent issues with friends. She didn't tell him his mistake.

'I've not been to Florence,' she said, determined to keep the conversation light. 'Would you recommend it?'

'It's a beautiful city, but it's best to go before it gets too hot. You ladies don't seem to be able to manage the heat. That's why we're going in January. And this time, it will help us put this awful business behind us.'

'Yes, it is quite frightful. Has the inspector spoken to either of you yet?'

'We've both given our statements, Gigi,' said Binky. His voice was lower than usual, as if he were growling a warning.

'I had to give the inspector an alibi,' replied Lady Gayle.

'As did we, Lady Gayle,' replied Piffers. 'Binky and I were at the shoot; we were next to each other, and so we can vouch for each other. I don't know about the other chaps.'

'I think it's the same for the chaps lower down the line,' replied Lady Gayle. 'They can all vouch for each other.'

'Good,' said Piffers. 'Then that counts us all out, even though we had guns to hand, we were none of us near the man. I certainly had no reason to shoot him. Never seen him before in my life.'

'I thought someone told me you and he were in the same regiment though?' Lady Gayle fluttered her eyelashes at him.

'Do you have any idea how many men are in a regiment, my dear lady?' said Piffers.

Having driven her ambulance on the Western Front during the Great War, Lady Gayle had an extremely good idea, but she chose to shake her head.

'Well, far too many for me to have known one individual who wasn't under my command.' Lord Hansen snorted and strode to the window, staring out into the garden.

'Didn't Jack Parsons box for your regiment?' said Lady Gayle, her face the picture of innocence. 'I thought he was the regimental champion.'

'I have no interest in boxing, my dear lady. Now, if you'll excuse me, I need to speak to my wife.' Lord Hansen nodded at his host and strode from the room.

'Well, that didn't go well, did it, Gigi?' Binky sniggered. 'No answers to your questions, and now you've upset him, he won't answer any more questions.'

'On the contrary, Binky,' said Lady Gayle. 'He's covering something up. I am quite sure that he did know the victim, and I am equally sure he would have seen the man box. Jack Parsons won the regimental championship. Lord Hansen, lover of boxing or not, would have had to support the regiment at the match. His attendance would have been expected if not mandatory. He knew the victim, Binky, I'm sure of it, and he's just lied about it.'

CHAPTER FOURTEEN

'Remind me never to lie to you,' said Binky.

Lady Gayle stared at him. 'Are you sure you haven't lied to me already, Binky?' she said, folding her arms. 'You told me that you had paid off all of your debts. Was that entirely true?'

'Now, I say,' blustered Binky. 'I was perfectly honest with you when I said I'd paid off all the debts I had before I was married.'

'You did indeed,' said Lady Gayle, she perched herself on the sofa facing him. 'What about since your marriage? Can you honestly tell me that you have no gambling debts now?'

Binky put his hands together as if in prayer, and then he linked his fingers, rubbing the top of one thumb against the base of the other. 'Well... I may have run up a few more debts recently.'

'Oh, Binky,' sighed Lady Gayle. 'Do you have any idea how much you owe?'

'Not exactly,' replied Binky. He unlinked his hands and

covered his face with them. 'It's quite a bit, but that's not the main problem.'

'So what *is* the main problem?' said Lady Gayle.

'I gave my IOUs to the Pope, and now they've been sold.' Binky furrowed his brow and pinched the bridge of his nose between thumb and forefinger.

'Your Mr Pope has sold them? Do you know to whom?'

'Not Mr Pope. *The* Pope,' corrected Binky. 'I believe they've been sold to a gangster called William Saffron. He is a nasty piece of work, and he employs people like Jack Parsons as enforcers.'

'When did you find that out?' said Lady Gayle.

'Just before Christmas,' sighed Binky. 'The Pope loaned me the money initially, but he did say if I was slow in paying up, he might have to sell my IOUs to someone else. It's a dashed nuisance as the Pope always used to be a gentleman and didn't harass one about one's debts.'

'So, you're telling me that this Pope character only *planned* to sell the IOUs, but now it appears as if he already *has* sold them.' Lady Gayle thought that the Pope sounded like he'd reached the end of this tether. If his debtors were not inclined to pay back the monies they owed, then selling the IOUs, even at a fraction of their face value, seemed a wise move.

'That's the only explanation for Parsons being here,' said Lord Ridgewell.

'When did you talk to him, Binky?'

'Who? Parsons? I didn't. I didn't know he was here until I saw his body. Gigi, you have to believe me.' Binky slapped his hands onto his knees and stood. He went to the drinks cabinet and poured himself a large whisky. He waggled the decanter at Lady Gayle.

She shook her head. 'A little early for me, Binky. I've

only just eaten lunch.' She sighed. 'You should tell the inspector. If you let him find this out for himself, he'll think you're guilty. If you confess all to him now, then it looks less like a tale you've made up. Don't forget you were with your gamekeeper all afternoon; you came straight back to the house and then spent some time with Bundle and me. Do you have any time that you cannot account for?'

Binky tossed the whisky down his throat and slammed the glass back on top of the drinks cabinet. 'No,' he said. 'I don't think there's any time when I wasn't with someone else.'

'Then you must tell the inspector,' hissed Lady Gayle.

'Tell the inspector what?' asked Inspector Coward as he strolled into the library. 'What is it you need to tell me, Lord Ridgewell?'

'Oh lor,' said Binky. 'That's torn it. I suppose I'd better tell you everything.'

'Is usually the best idea, my lord,' said Inspector Coward. 'I always find that honesty is very much the best policy. Especially in a murder case.'

Binky flopped onto the sofa with a thump. When he glanced up at Lady Gayle, she had the distinct feeling that he looked like a trapped rat. He was sweating, his rounded eyes darting to every corner of the library, searching for an escape route.

'Come clean, Binky. Tell him about the debts,' she whispered. 'You've got alibis. No one can accuse you of this murder.'

Inspector Coward coughed, and Lady Gayle glared at him.

'It would be best if Lord Ridgewell and I spoke alone, my lady,' said the inspector.

Lady Gayle folded her arms as she turned to face him. The inspector shrugged and took his notebook from his pocket.

'How much debt are you in, Lord Ridgewell?' began Inspector Coward.

Binky shook his head. 'I have no idea,' he replied. 'I don't have copies of the IOUs, and since I was probably three sheets to the wind when I signed them, I won't have noted the amounts down. The Pope detailed them to me in letters. He wanted promissory notes as they were more legally binding.'

'I see,' said the inspector. 'However, I don't think even a promissory note would be legally binding for illegal gambling.'

'Do you mean that they can't be enforced in a court of law?' Binky began to look hopeful.

'No, my lord, not enforceable in the courts. That's why gangsters such as Mr Saffron use their own form of enforcement, people like the victim, Mr Parsons. Gangsters don't tend to reply on the law when pressing for debt repayments. They have their own laws.'

Binky paled. 'I didn't see Parsons when he was here. I promise you, Inspector. I never saw him.'

'As you say, my lord, but I can't just take your word for it, can I?'

'Why can't you? I'm a gentleman, dash it all, man. I'm not used to being spoken to like this.'

'I'm sure you're not, Lord Ridgewell. I'm sure you're not.' Inspector Coward's face was as impassive as any good butler. It was impossible to gauge from his expression what he was really thinking.

Lady Gayle thought he'd make rather a good poker player. She looked from one man to the other. 'I think you'll find, Inspector,' she said. 'That Lord Ridgewell can account for all of his movements and can produce people to vouch for him all afternoon.'

'I've spoken to the staff already,' said Inspector Coward. 'But I don't place much stock in their answers. They are always going to vouch for the gentry. Always have done and always will.'

'My staff are honest people,' replied Binky with a sniff. 'They will always tell the truth.'

'If you say so, my lord. It has not been my experience with all domestic staff, but if you say so. Now, the shoot began after lunch?'

'Yes,' said Binky. 'We set off around one o'clock because of the short afternoon. My man, Snelling, ensured that we had refreshments at three o'clock, and we shot for a little longer, but the light was fading. At around four, it became unsafe as the light was going, and we headed back to the house.'

'Were all the shooting party there?'

'I think so,' said Binky. 'I didn't take rollcall. My gamekeeper took the shotguns back, and they went into his office to be locked up. We don't like leaving guns around loose since there can be accidents.'

'Quite so, my lord,' said the inspector. 'However, the shooting of Mr Parsons was no accident.'

There was a knock at the door, and Inspector Coward frowned as one of his constables rushed into the room. He sped to his senior officer, sat, and whispered in the inspector's ear.

The inspector's jaw tightened for a fraction of a second. He rose, 'We'll have to continue this later, my lord,' he said.

'Lady Gayle, I would still like your maid to look at Mr Parsons' body, but in the meantime, something has come up which needs my immediate attention.'

He nodded at both Lord Ridgewell and Lady Gayle and strode from the room.

CHAPTER FIFTEEN

'What do you suppose all that was about?' said Binky. Then he frowned, 'and why does your maid need to look at the body?'

'In answer to the first question, I expect they've found some new evidence,' replied Lady Gayle. 'As for the second? Well, Alice saw someone who should not have been in the house. It may have been the victim.

'But Binky, while the inspector is otherwise engaged, we do need to get to the bottom of how much you owe this William Saffron. Have you got any information? Notes or letters? Anything so that we can make a start?'

'My study,' said Binky, pouring himself another whisky. 'Anything that I have will be in there.'

'Very well,' said Lady Gayle, getting to her feet. She strode to the door in a purposeful manner. 'Let's make a start.'

To say that Binky's papers were in a mess would be polite. Lady Gayle thought of her desk at Bethencourt Castle and how Harry Howden kept her papers and the estate accounts straight. She was still learning and didn't have a complete grasp of how the estate was run, but she did hope, as she took on greater command of her affairs, that her desk would look as if everything were under control.

Binky placed sheaves of paper on the blotting-pad in front of her. He had ceded his desk and chair to her. As Binky paced the room, Lady Gayle flattened the letters out and started working through them, trying to gain some semblance of order. Each letter from the Pope she put into a separate pile. Anything related to the estate went in another stack, and bills she placed in a third pile.

Going through the letters from the Pope, Lady Gayle found herself curious about what kind of man would loan people money to gamble away. The rate of interest wasn't high, only a little more than the Bank of England base rate. She was still learning about the rates of interest on loans, but she always thought they were scandalous. She noted the numbers down one after another.

'Where do you do your gambling, Binky?' she said.

'At The 43 Club. You know, 43 Gerrard Street.' he replied.

'Do you go there often?'

'No, not anymore. I can't afford to, and now there's a sprog on the way, things are going to be even tighter.'

Lady Gayle nodded and began to tot up the numbers. When she had a total, she whistled and went through her numbers again. Just to be certain, she went through the numbers a third time. The total didn't change, and the amount astounded her. She was confident that if this much were taken from her estate in one lump sum, she would be bankrupt.

'How did you plan to pay this back, Binky?' she said, checking her figures a fourth time.

'Sell the family silver, perhaps. There's a Gainsborough in the main hall, a minor work, but I should get a few bob for it. There's some land that I could sell off too.' He sighed as he turned to face her. 'Have you worked out the dreaded number yet?'

'Yes, Binky,' she said. 'I've checked it four times. As far as I can see from these figures here, you owe just over ten thousand pounds.'

'Gosh,' said Binky. He exhaled and plonked himself onto a chair. 'It's going to take a bit more than the family silver, then,' he said.

'Is there any jewellery?' asked Lady Gayle.

'Mama's diamonds are in a safe box at the bank. They might fetch a few bob too. I didn't realise it was that much, you know.'

'Well, you're more than welcome to check my numbers, but it does give you a very good motive for killing Jack Parsons if he was here to squeeze money out of you. Do you keep much money here in the house?'

Binky shook his head. 'A hundred pounds or so,' he said. 'More or less. Snelling may have some cash below stairs to pay off local tradesmen, but I can't see that being more than a few guineas. Am I in dreadful trouble?'

'I should say so, Binky. This amount of debt is the last thing you'd want Bundle to find out about, isn't it?'

'Too right,' agreed Binky. 'I promised her no more debts.'

'Why do you do it, then? I've seen you play, you're no poker player.'

'No, I know I'm not. Unlike Charles,' he sighed. 'Charles actually makes money from playing cards, among other things. It's all about the excitement for me, I suppose. It makes me feel alive.'

'Well, you're not the gambler Charles is, are you?' said Lady Gayle. She thought back to Charles' change in mood earlier and wondered if Lord Vickery was involved in more than simple gambling. 'You're going to have to find your excitement elsewhere from now on. No more gambling for you, Binky.'

'I know you're right.' Binky sighed heavily, leaning back in his chair. 'Perhaps I could do some sleuthing, like you?'

Lady Gayle looked at him, the picture of misery and defeat. Poor Bundle, she thought. Aloud, she said, 'You said Charles makes money from gambling "among other things". What other things, Binky? Do you know, or are you guessing?'

'What do you know about his escapades in Atlantic City?'

Lady Gayle shook her head. 'Only that he left in a hurry. I always assumed he was supplying illegal alcohol.'

Binky gave a harsh laugh. 'Definitely booze, but I hear that he was supplying other party favours too.'

'Drugs, you mean?' Lady Gayle was well aware of Charles' involvement in supplying cocaine to his friends. He had, after all, once supplied her. At least until she saw the error of her ways.

Binky nodded and took another swig of his whisky.

'Is there anything else you're not telling me?'

'No, there's nothing else.'

Lady Gayle narrowed her eyes at Binky. 'The Pope, did you always meet him in person? What was he like?'

'Not top drawer, but I still think public school. Not a top-notch one, but he's got money.'

'Any ideas as to where he got his money from?'

'None at all.'

'And you're sure it was his money? You don't think he was acting for someone else?'

It was Binky's turn to squint at Lady Gayle. 'Acting for someone? But who?'

Lady Gayle pursed her lips, wondering if this was another way Charles was making money. *Could Charles be The Pope?* He had been behind her when Jackie Parsons was uncovered. Was it Charles she'd heard gasp? She shook her head, trying to rid herself of the treacherous thought. No, please, not Charles, she told herself.

Returning to the matter in hand, she said, 'Binky, I can't see how you're ever going to pay this off. You must have been mad to let it get this out of hand.'

Binky covered his face with his hands. 'Bundle will kill me if she finds out,' he muttered in a forlorn voice.

'Quite possibly, but there's no *if*. I rather think Bundle knows exactly what's been going on. She's no fool,' replied Lady Gayle. 'Now tell me exactly what you got up to on New Year's Eve. From going to the shoot, tell me everything you did step by step and don't miss anything out.'

With a pout, Binky took another gulp of whisky and went through his movements of the fateful afternoon. Lady Gayle listened and made notes. Unlike Inspector Coward, who she knew had taught himself shorthand, her notes were painstakingly laborious. But when she read them back to Binky and asked if he could remember anything else, he could not.

'Well, I can't see how you would have had time to shoot Mr Parsons, disrobe him and hide him in the bonfire, but that's not to say Inspector Coward will come to the same conclusion. What about everyone else? Where were they?'

'I'm going to need time to think about that,' said Binky.

'I know Piffers and Vickers were with me as we walked back together. Artie had disappeared, and so had Pongo, but I have a pretty good idea where Pongo was.' He winked at her, and Lady Gayle, remembering the gossip from Charles Vickery, shuddered.

'You think it has to be one of us chaps, don't you?' said Binky. 'You don't suspect any of the ladies?'

'Would any of the ladies have a motive to shoot Mr Parsons?' Lady Gayle raised her eyebrows at Binky. Although she still wondered how Mrs Bishop had known the age of the victim. She decided she needed to speak to that lady further. 'Apart from the fact that they were all together in the drawing or sitting room keeping Bundle company. The man was shot with a shotgun, so that's not something a lady can hide easily about her person. Also, someone had to carry the victim to the bonfire and hide him inside it. Can you see any of the ladies carrying a full-grown man?'

Binky shook his head. 'It was worth a try,' he said.

'We're going to have to try harder, Binky,' said Lady Gayle. 'You have a child on the way. You're not going to be a very good father if you've already been taken by the hangman, are you?'

Binky hung his head and plunged his hands deep into his pockets, the picture of misery.

CHAPTER SIXTEEN

LADY GAYLE LEFT BINKY IN HIS STUDY AND MADE HER WAY TO THE drawing room. As she crossed the hall, the grandfather clock struck four and two maids crossed the foyer bringing large trays for afternoon tea.

As if in response to the sight of the tea trays, her stomach rumbled. She pressed her hand against her tummy, trying to quell the noise whilst wondering why investigations always made her so hungry. Probably all that brain work, she decided.

Snelling opened the door for her as she passed into the drawing room. Lady Gayle glanced up at him, wondering what he had seen and could or would tell. Like all old retainers, he would be loyal to the family as Inspector Coward had already suggested, but would he let his master get away with murder? It was hard to tell. She was quite sure that, loyal as her staff were, if she'd committed a crime as heinous as murder, they would want to see justice done.

After she had taken a cup of tea and some sandwiches from the tray, Lady Gayle made her way to where Mrs Bishop was sitting.

'Dreadful business all this, isn't it,' said Lady Gayle, dropping into a seat near her target.

'Yes,' replied the other. 'Quite dreadful. I don't think my John would have liked me to be mixed up in anything like this. It would have made him very upset.'

'Yes, I fully understand,' said Lady Gayle. 'I am sure that my late husband would have felt the same.' She didn't really believe that. Hugh would have thought it all great fun and would have more than likely encouraged her, but she didn't think that would be the right tactic to take with Mrs Bishop.

Mrs Bishop didn't respond to the remark but simply drank more of her tea. Oh well, here goes, thought Lady Gayle. 'I don't suppose you knew the young man, did you?'

'Well, of course not. What kind of a question is that?' Mrs Bishop slammed her teacup onto the table, and all the other ladies turned to stare at the cause of the upset.

'I am sorry,' said Lady Gayle. 'It's just that my maid thinks she saw a young man in the corridor where our bedrooms are on the afternoon of New Year's Eve. I simply wondered if you had seen him too?'

'I rather think your maid has flights of fancy,' said Mrs Bishop. 'Now, if you'll excuse me, I have quite lost my appetite.'

She swept from the room in a manner that, Lady Gayle was sure, even *her* mother would have been proud.

AFTER TEA, Lady Gayle retired to her room to lie down and rest before dinner. She had popped in to see Bundle, who was uncomfortable but perfectly fine. Binky was having tea with her, and Lady Gayle decided to leave husband and wife alone. They had quite a lot to discuss.

When Lady Gayle entered her own room, she was relieved to see Alice hard at work taking care of her clothes, 'I am so pleased to see a friendly face,' she said, flopping onto the bed. 'I tried talking to Mrs Bishop about the young man you saw. She nearly bit my head off. She says there was no young man in the corridor and that you imagined it.'

'Yes, milady,' Alice sniffed. 'I am well known for my overactive imagination.'

Lady Gayle squinted at her maid for a moment. It was unlike Alice to be quite so acerbic. She was normally a very calm person, even if her views of people were occasionally a little harsh. 'Are you quite well, Alice?' she said. 'Put those things down. Sit here and tell me everything.' She patted a spot beside her on the bed, and Alice, after a sigh, complied.

'I didn't imagine anyone in the corridor, milady,' Alice began. 'I thought he was outside Mrs Bishop's door, but it may have been Lady Ridgewell's instead. There's uproar downstairs as everyone is convinced that someone else killed the young man—'

'His name was Jack Parsons,' said Lady Gayle. 'He had been a champion boxer. Inspector Coward says he was working for a London gangster who was a money lender.'

'Is that why he was here, milady?' asked Alice.

'Working for his gangster boss? Yes, it's very possible, Alice. However, I do have something to ask you,' said Lady Gayle. 'I told Inspector Coward that you'd seen someone, and now he'd like you to take a look at the body to see if it's the same person. Will you do that, Alice? I wouldn't ask if it weren't important, but no one can make you if you don't want to.'

'I can't say as I'm happy with that, milady, but if you think it will help?' Alice's voice cracked as she spoke. 'When will I need to do it?'

'I think Mr Parsons may have been taken to the hospital mortuary, so not for a day or two, and I wouldn't let you do it on your own. I'll be with you all the time.' Lady Gayle squeezed Alice's hand.

'Very well, milady, but you don't need to be with me. I can manage,' said Alice. 'Now, would you like to hear what else I've discovered?'

'Oh, yes, please,' said Lady Gayle.

Alice rose and continued tidying clothes. 'Well, there is a lot of talk about Lord and Lady Hansen. Their marriage is not a happy one by all accounts. There's other talk about his lordship, but that's not something I want to discuss.' Alice glanced at Lady Gayle, her face stricken.

Lady Gayle could guess what the talk was. 'Carry on.'

'Then there's talk about Sir William and about Lord Collins too. Did you know he was court-martialled?'

'Who? Lord Collins? I didn't know about that,' said Lady Gayle. She sat up and pulled her pillows behind her to make herself more comfortable. 'Does anyone know why?'

'It's a big secret,' whispered Alice. 'All very hush-hush, but I think Mr Snelling has a good idea. Lord Collins' man knows too, but obviously, no one wants to discuss it in front of him. He likes Lord Collins and won't hear a word said against him. He says Lord Collins is worth more than a lot of the young men here.'

'Does his lordship's valet have anything to say about Lady Collins?'

Alice shook her head. 'He just says that she's a nice, kind mistress. Her maid says the same. But I don't think Lord and Lady Collins are very happy. They want children, and none have made an appearance.'

Gosh, more babies, thought Lady Gayle. *Everyone is*

obsessed with babies. Aloud, she said, 'Lord Collins was missing from the shoot later in the afternoon.'

'Oh, my lady, you can't possibly think it was Lord Collins who shot the man, can you?'

'I don't know at the moment,' replied Lady Gayle. I don't seem to be able to think straight. Let's go through the suspects.'

'Yes, milady,' said Alice. 'Will you want your notebook?'

'Yes, please,' replied Lady Gayle, 'but first, where did you see the young man? Go to the door and tell me which door he was outside.'

Alice opened the bedroom door and peered down the corridor. She turned to face Lady Gayle. 'It's hard to tell, milady,' she said.

Lady Gayle edged past her and peered out into the passageway. 'I'll pretend to be him, and you can tell me when to stop.' She walked down the corridor until Alice hissed at her that she was in the right place.

Far from being outside Mrs Bishop's room, if the place that Alice indicated was the correct one, Mr Parsons had been standing exactly outside Bundle's bedroom.

'Dash it all,' said Lady Gayle as she ran back to her room. She'd heard Binky on the other side of the door and did not want to be found in the corridor. After their conversation, she did not want him to think she was pointing the finger of suspicion at him. However, she had to be honest with herself. Things were not looking good for her host.

CHAPTER SEVENTEEN

Pushing the unpleasant thought aside, Lady Gayle decided to speak with Artie Collins and set out in search of him. If her preliminary search failed, she knew she could ask Snelling. Like her own butler, Fredericks, Snelling always knew exactly where everyone was.

However, having searched all the rooms on the ground floor, Lady Gayle had to give in and ask Snelling where the erstwhile peer was.

'I do believe that he asked if he could take a look at the wine cellar, my lady,' replied Snelling. 'Lord Ridgewell was happy to give permission, and the gentleman set off half an hour ago. You may want to take a coat with you, my lady. It can be very cold down there.'

'Thank you,' replied Lady Gayle. She collected a shawl from her room, and with Alice hot on her heels, they inched down the stone steps into the cellars under St Nesban's House.

. . .

At first, it was quiet in the vault, apart from the clop of their heels on the stone floor. Snelling had shown Lady Gayle where the switches were for the electric light, but Alice was carrying a lantern as a backup. On either side of the corridors lay bottle upon bottle of wine laid down by previous generations of Ridgewells. Here's another source of income for Binky, thought Lady Gayle, although she hoped that he would not need to sell everything off. So many estates were being broken up and sold off to meet the demands of high post-war taxes. It was one of her greatest fears about the Bethencourt estate.

Lady Gayle hesitated for a moment, her head cocked to one side. She held her hand up to halt their progress, signalling to Alice not to make a sound. Holding her breath, she heard the soft noise again. It was the clicking sound of a revolver cylinder being snapped back into the main frame of the gun and spun. The hammer dropping could be heard, too, albeit more faintly. She glanced at Alice and placed a finger over her lips. Alice nodded, and together, they moved closer to the sound.

Lord Arthur Collins sat on a low stack of wine boxes with his old service revolver. Lady Gayle was pleased to see that there was no ammunition in sight. She gulped when Artie whirled around and pointed the business end of the revolver at them both.

'Artie,' she said, raising her hands, 'It's just me, Gigi. My maid and I were worried about you. No one has seen you for ages, so we decided to come and find you.'

'Is there a search party?' Lord Collins held the gun away from them and pointed it towards a beer barrel. Holding the revolver up, he spun the cylinder with his right hand and pulled the trigger. The hammer dropped, and Lady

Gayle held her hands over her ears, but there was no explosion.

Shaking, she pulled her shoulders back and cleared her throat. 'Why don't you come upstairs, Artie? Just you and me? Come along, and we can have a nice cup of tea together.' Lady Gayle hated the sound of her whining voice. However, at the mention of tea, Artie rose.

'Confound it,' he said. 'You know, I *am* quite thirsty. I didn't think to bring anything with me.'

Lady Gayle held out her hand to him as if he were a child she was going to lead back to a party.

Artie glanced at her hand, putting his own out to take hers. Then he shook his head and flopped down on the wine boxes once more. 'Is the policeman still here?' he said.

'He's not looking for you, Artie. He's talking to Lord Ridgewell,' replied Lady Gayle. She had no idea where the inspector was, but the very idea of him finding Artie whilst he was in this confused state would do his lordship no good at all.

Lord Collins placed his hand in his jacket pocket and removed a bullet, which he placed in the revolver's cylinder.

'Milady,' hissed Alice. 'We should go. We need to get help. It's far too dangerous down here.'

Lady Gayle waved her hand impatiently. She was convinced that Artie would be fine if only he would talk. 'Tell me about the shooting party,' she said. 'Did you bag many pheasants?'

'A couple,' replied Artie. 'My heart wasn't in it. Piffers had been beastly to me earlier in the day.'

'Why would Piffers be like that?' asked Lady Gayle.

'He's always been beastly,' replied Artie. 'Ever since

prep school. He was still a sneak when we moved up to Brampton. I hoped it was something he'd grow out of, but he didn't.'

'Artie, I'm sorry. I don't understand. Apart from the outburst at cards, Piffers always seems so kind and friendly.'

Lord Collins laughed harshly. It sounded more like a snarl. 'I told you, he's a dirty sneak and a tattle tale,' repeated Artie. 'I hated him.'

Lady Gayle sighed, thinking it was a jolly good job that it wasn't Piffers who'd been killed. 'Did you see Mr Parsons on the day he was shot, Artie? Or perhaps Piffers did?'

Lord Collins shrugged and slipped to the floor. A bottle rolled away, and Lady Gayle realised that his lordship, despite saying he'd brought no refreshments with him, had been making free with Binky's wine whilst he'd hidden himself in the cellar. She only hoped that it was not one of the best vintages.

'Perhaps we should go upstairs and get that cup of tea. I'll ask Lady Collins to take care of you. Or perhaps Alice could fetch your man?'

Artie nodded, and Lady Gayle turned to her maid. 'Alice, could you fetch Lord Collins' valet? Tell him that his lordship is a little worse for wear and needs some assistance.'

'I don't like leaving you down here with him like this, milady. Not when he's got a gun,' Alice whispered.

'Leave me the lantern,' said Lady Gayle, glancing at Artie, who was too drunk to notice their conversation. 'If he points the gun at me, I'll throw it at him.'

Alice glowered but passed the lantern to her mistress. Her rapid footsteps could be heard echoing in the cellar as they faded away.

'Said he was going to tell everyone why he thought I was a coward.' Artie slurred as he wobbled precariously. The wine boxes shifted under his weight. His voice was so low that Lady Gayle needed to edge closer to him to hear his words.

'I'm sure you're not a coward,' she said. 'I'm sure you were very brave. I'm sure you were as brave as any of your friends.'

Artie snarled his harsh laugh again. 'Piffers said he'd tell everyone. I had to do exactly as he said, or he'd tell everybody.'

'Tell everyone what?' said Lady Gayle. A sound behind her made her twist around. She thought that Alice had been very quick in finding the valet, but all she saw was the ground rushing up to meet her.

'My lady, my lady.' Snelling's anxious voice broke through the haze, and Lady Gayle sat up slowly, holding her aching head.

'Gigi, are you all right?' called Binky.

'I'm fine,' she said, trying to stand. Her knees gave way, and she resumed her position on the floor. 'Where's Artie? I was here talking to Artie.'

'It's too late, my lady.' Inspector Coward's voice broke through the cacophony of voices. 'I'm afraid Lord Collins has shot himself.'

Lady Gayle held out her hand, and Inspector Coward pulled her to her feet. She grabbed hold of his arm and clenched it tightly as she peered over the stack of wine boxes on the floor.

Artie lay on the ground, his right hand gripping his revolver and his head surrounded by blood.

'Oh, Artie, you fool,' she said, bringing her hand to her mouth. Tears pricked her eyes, and she batted them away furiously. 'You absolute fool.'

CHAPTER EIGHTEEN

Lady Gayle took one last glance at Artie's body, and then, head bowed, she allowed herself to be led away from the distressing scene by Alice and Bundle's maid, Mary, who had been asked by Lord Ridgewell to help Alice guide Lady Gayle back to her bedroom.

Lady Gayle was unable to believe she had been so close to getting Artie to tell her something. *He had been on the point of telling me the truth, hadn't he? Why did he choose to take his own life at that point?* She shook her head and then held on tightly to both maids as her head spun and her vision blurred.

'That's quite a nasty knock on the head he gave you, milady,' said Alice. 'It's a good job he killed himself, or I would have swung for him.'

'And got yourself the sack,' hissed Mary.

'I know,' replied Alice, 'but I'm that upset at seeing my lady hurt.'

'Don't worry, Alice, I'm still here,' said Lady Gayle. She reached out to squeeze Alice's hand whilst biting back a chuckle at Alice's fierce protectiveness. *Oh my goodness, how my head hurts. How did he hit me? When did he hit me? I don't remember him moving.* She frowned, trying to revisit the scene in her mind, but it was all such a blur. She needed time to think.

Once back in the hallway, she braced herself for the stairs to her bedroom. All she wanted to do was go to sleep, but even with her limited medical knowledge, she suspected that there was a chance of concussion, and she knew that the doctor would insist she stay awake for some hours to come. Hopefully, it would give her the thinking time she desperately needed.

Alice sat her down in the armchair by the fire and placed a blanket over her knees. 'Would you like some tea, milady?' she asked.

'I think just some water, please, Alice,' Lady Gayle replied.

'The doctor will come upstairs to check you over, but he is taking care of Lord Collins' body just now. Inspector Coward has already been to ask after your health.'

'Thank you, Alice. Perhaps I could talk to Inspector Coward after I have spoken with the doctor?'

'Very good, milady.' Alice placed the glass of water on a side table well within her ladyship's reach and left to go to her sewing in the dressing room. Whatever else happened, Lady Gayle knew that Alice would stay close at hand in case she was needed.

Lady Gayle sipped some water and held a damp handkerchief to her head. Gingerly, she traced her fingers over the lump that was forming on the back of her head. *It's on the back of your head, Gayle. How on earth did Artie hit you on the back of your head? He was in front of you.* She knew it made no sense, but nothing did at that moment. She closed her eyes, and immediately Alice was beside her.

'Is there anything I can get for you, milady?' her maid's eyes were full of concern. Clearly, even though Alice had secreted herself in the adjoining room, she was keeping a close eye on her mistress.

'I'm perfectly fine, Alice,' replied Lady Gayle, patting her on the hand. 'I just closed my eyes for a second.' She looked towards the door where she'd heard a knock. Alice opened the door, and the local general practitioner strolled in.

'How are you, your ladyship?' he said. 'Took quite a knock on the head, I understand?'

'Yes, doctor,' replied Lady Gayle, she indicated the lump on her head.

The doctor gave it a quick glance but shone his light in her eyes. 'You must have a very thick skull,' he said. 'No signs of concussion, but probably best not to drop off for a while.'

'Do I have to stay in my room, doctor?'

'It may be for the best,' he said. 'Everyone else is dressing for dinner. Are you hungry? Would you like dinner?'

Lady Gayle shook her head and winced again. 'I should really stop doing that,' she said, touching her fingertips to her temple.

'I think rest is the best idea, but if you want to go and sit with other people, that should be fine. Just don't get bored and drop off. If your headaches get particularly bad, you can call me back. I understand that you were with the gentleman when he shot himself?'

'Yes, doctor, but I didn't see anything. He hit me on the head before he shot himself. I suppose he didn't want me to stop him.'

The doctor frowned for a moment and took another look at the lump on the back of her head. 'That's certainly a possibility,' he said. 'You should be right as rain in a day or two. But if you feel sleepy, get up and walk around for a bit. We don't want you slipping into a coma, do we?'

'The police inspector wants to question me,' Lady Gayle said.

'That's fine, so long as you feel up to it. Don't let him bully you though; I know what these police inspectors are like.' The doctor placed his torch and stethoscope back in his Gladstone bag. 'I'll come back and give you the once over this evening,' he said.

NO SOONER HAD he gone than there was another knock on the door, and Inspector Coward burst into the room. 'I came as soon as they would let me in,' he gasped. 'I've been rather worried about you. How badly are you hurt?'

'I believe I am well enough to answer some questions, Inspector,' Lady Gayle said. She was somewhat surprised by this outburst and pushed herself up in the armchair. Alice moved forward and placed herself between her mistress and the policeman while she plumped up the cushions.

'Well, yes, I do have some questions,' said Inspector Coward, 'but I was concerned about you too. You always seem to be putting yourself in danger.'

'It's not something I seek out, Inspector,' said Lady Gayle. 'I was talking with Artie, and then I was hit on the head.'

'What were you talking about?' the inspector edged back and sat in the armchair on the other side of the fire.

'You know,' said Lady Gayle with a frown. 'I'm not really sure. He wasn't admitting to the murder, if that's what you want to know. He was talking more about Piffers—Lord

Hansen. There was some animosity between them, but Artie didn't get time to tell me what that was.'

'Bad blood between him and Lord Hansen, you say?' Inspector Coward whipped his notebook out, and the pencil raced across the surface.

'Lord Collins said that Lord Hansen called him a coward—'

'Well, suicide is considered the coward's way out—'

'You know, I've never had much time for that idea,' said Lady Gayle. 'I think it takes a lot of bravery to place a gun against your head and pull the trigger. It's not the act of a coward at all.' Lady Gayle cradled her chin and glared at the inspector. 'I don't know what the problem between Piffers and Artie was, but there was definitely something going on.'

'I'll speak with Lady Collins,' replied Inspector Coward.

'Good idea,' said Lady Gayle, wondering how much notice Pamela Collins paid to her own husband's concerns. She glanced at Alice. *She knows all my secrets, if you wanted to know anything about me, Alice would be the person to ask.*

Wondering who knew Artie's secrets, Lady Gayle bade farewell to the inspector. She felt the bump on the back of her head once more. 'Alice, she said, 'how well do you know Lord Collins' valet?'

CHAPTER NINETEEN

After a light breakfast the next morning, Lady Gayle followed Alice as she led the way from the east wing to the west wing where Lord Collins had had his bedroom. She wandered along, still feeling a little lightheaded, although the swelling on her head had shrunk considerably. Alice knocked on the door, and when a young man opened it, he beckoned them both inside.

'This is Victor, milady. He's Lord Collins' valet.'

'Hello, Victor,' said Lady Gayle. 'Let me say how sorry I am for your loss.'

'Thank you, milady,' replied Victor, 'Alice said you wanted a word. How can I help you?'

'How long have you been with Artie, I mean Lord Collins?'

'I was his batman in the Great War, milady,' Victor dipped his head, and Lady Gayle saw a tear blot the tie Victor was folding. He put the tie to one side and accepted the handkerchief that Alice produced from her apron pocket.

'That must have been a terrible time,' sympathised Lady Gayle. 'I was an ambulance driver.'

'Very brave, milady, I must say,' replied Victor with a sniff worthy of his late master. 'You didn't have to be at the front. We were soldiers, it was our duty, but *you* didn't have to be there.'

'We all wanted to do our bit. I don't think I would have been a good nurse.'

Victor flashed her a smile. 'I'm sure you would have been wonderful, milady,' he said. 'When his lordship was in hospital, all the nurses were very kind.'

'I didn't realise that Artie had been injured,' said Lady Gayle. She glanced at Alice, who gave a brief shake of her head.

'Mustard gas, milady,' supplied Victor. 'That's why he was left with that sniff. Terrible damage to his lungs, and you should have seen his poor body. Covered in blisters, he was. The scars he was left with are, sorry, were quite dreadful. He was a lovely man was, Lord Collins, but later, he said that using gas took all the chivalry out of war.

'He hated the Hun after that. We all hated them, but after the mustard gas was used, Lord Collins changed. He'd been doing his duty before the gas attacks, but afterwards... well afterwards, he really hated them. He despised them, and he wanted revenge.'

'How did he get along with the other officers in the regiment?' asked Lady Gayle.

'I don't think there were any problems, milady. At least not until after he'd been in hospital.'

'What changed after he had been hospitalised?'

'The nightmares, milady. He'd wake everyone up with his screaming, and that wasn't liked. It gave everyone the jitters. His lordship kept saying that he could smell gas, and he'd ask for the gas gong to be sounded. That was the warning sound, milady.'

Lady Gayle nodded. She remembered the gas gong. Just a tin plate and a wooden spoon, however, hit rapidly with enough force the sound was ear-splitting. She touched her fingertips to her head. Even the memory was making her head hurt now.

'That's when the rumours started, milady,' Victor flushed and dipped his head.

'Rumours?' said Lady Gayle.

'They said he was a coward, milady. Said he kept sounding the warning gong so he didn't have to leave his dugout.'

'Oh, poor Artie,' said Lady Gayle. There had been days when she'd not wanted to get in her ambulance and drive to the front, but at least each night, she returned to the comparative safety of the hospital. Sleeping in a room dug into the side of the trenches in the thick of the combat would have been terrifying. 'He must have been very unhappy.'

'It just made things worse, milady. When they all refused to speak to him, he gave up. I couldn't get him to come out of his room. Then it got worse.'

'How could it get worse, Victor? It already sounds quite dreadful,' said Lady Gayle.

'There was a court-martial, milady. His lordship was found guilty of cowardice and was going to the firing squad.' Victor faced away from her, his concentration entirely on brushing down his lordship's clothes.

Lady Gayle gasped and sat down on the ottoman. Artie had said he'd been called a coward and that Piffers was going to let everyone know why. "He said I had to do what he wanted, or he'd tell everyone," she recalled Artie's words from their last conversation. 'What happened after that?' asked Lady Gayle.

'I'm not sure, milady. Lord Collins disappeared from the camp, and I was moved to a new officer. Lord Collins was never mentioned again. I didn't know he was still alive until I sent his father my condolences. I didn't realise the old lord had died and I got a letter from Lord Collins offering me a job. I've been with him ever since.

'He was a lovely man,' said Victor. 'I don't think I'll find another placement with such a kind gentleman.' The valet coughed. It seemed as if he were trying to cover up the sound of his sobs, and Lady Gayle rose, feeling rather embarrassed.

'Thank you, Victor,' she said. 'You've been very helpful.'

Alice opened the door, and Lady Gayle slipped out into the corridor. 'I think I'd like a lie down,' she said to Alice.

'Yes, milady,' said Alice. 'The inspector wants me to look at the body later today. He wants to be sure that it's the same man as I saw in the afternoon.'

'Gosh, yes. I had completely forgotten. Later, you say?'

'Yes, milady.'

'I was going to come with you.'

'That will not be necessary, milady. Don't you worry about me.'

They continued making their way along the corridor, down the steps at the top of the main stairs and up the matching flight to the corridor leading to the blue room.

Once inside the bedroom, Alice said, 'What did we learn from Victor, milady? Was any of what he told us useful?'

'We've learnt that Lord Collins was accused of cowardice and wasn't executed for it as was normal. He escaped somehow, Alice. That's one thing, and it appears Piffers knew about it, which is the second thing, and finally, I believe, from the conversation I had with Lord Collins, Lord Hansen used that knowledge to make Artie do something against his will.'

'Could Lord Hansen really have forced Lord Collins to kill Mr Parsons?'

'I don't know Alice, I really don't. All I can say is that Lord Collins told me that Lord Hansen had threatened him with exposure of his secret unless he did what Lord Hansen wanted.'

'And the only thing that has happened is the murder,' said Alice. 'I thought you were going to ask Victor if Lord Collins had ruined any of his clothes?'

'I was Alice, but didn't you notice what Victor was brushing?'

'Milady?' Alice gave her a quizzical look.

'He was brushing a waistcoat. I saw this twig fall onto the floor while Victor was brushing it down.'

'When on earth did you pick that up, milady?'

'When I sat on the ottoman. I would have put money on you spotting what I was up to. Now I know it was Artie I saw rushing up the stairs, and now I have a horrid feeling I know exactly what he had been up to.' Lady Gayle dropped into the armchair by the fire and brushed her fingertips over the lump on the back of her head.

If only it would stop hurting so much, she thought, then I could think more clearly.

CHAPTER TWENTY

Alice rinsed out a cloth in the water bowl and laid it across Lady Gayle's head. 'Perhaps you should rest on the bed a little, milady,' she said. 'Do you have a headache?'

'Just a small one,' replied Lady Gayle. She took Alice's hand and allowed herself to be walked to the bed. 'I'm sure it will pass. I would like some sleep, though, after staying awake all night to prove I wasn't going to fall into a coma.' She laid down and closed her eyes, resting her head on the pillow.

'I was only doing what the doctor said I was to do.' Alice's tone scolded her, although her eyes were full of concern.

'I would love to sleep,' replied Lady Gayle. 'I feel very tired, but my mind is racing. I'm not sure that I could rest even if I tried.'

'Perhaps you should try? The inspector is expecting me to go to the mortuary in a little while. He's sending a constable for me.'

Lady Gayle yawned and nodded. 'Yes, of course. Are you sure you don't want me to come with you?' She propped herself up on her elbow. 'If you want me to go with you, I shall be tickety boo in a trice.'

Alice gave her a sceptical glance. 'No, milady. I think it's more important that you rest for a while.'

'Yes, perhaps you're right. The light is a little bright though.'

'I'll draw the curtains,' replied Alice. She looked out the window for a moment before drawing the heavy drapes across the glass. 'Tell me, milady, what can you recall after I left you alone with Lord Collins?'

Lady Gayle laid her head on the pillow again and closed her eyes, replaying the scene in her head. 'He was tossing that stupid gun from hand to hand. Then, pointing it at the wine barrel.'

'When he hit you, did he move too fast for you to stop him?'

Lady Gayle sat up and frowned. Alice plumped up the pillows behind her.

'I didn't see him move at all,' Lady Gayle said. 'Which means.' She stared at Alice, realisation dawning.

'It can't have been Lord Collins who hit you, can it?'

'Someone else must have been there,' said Lady Gayle. She closed one eye, wincing in pain. 'Alice, did you see Artie's body? I mean, did you see him after he'd been shot? Did you see which hand he had the gun in?'

'I only had a quick glance, milady. The inspector stood in the way, so I couldn't see anything. The gun was on the ground.' Alice closed her eyes, her hands moving as if she was tracing the scene. 'I think the gun was on the right side of his body, but that could have been where it fell. I'm sorry, milady. It all happened so quickly, and I was more worried about you.'

'Don't worry, Alice, I'm sure the inspector meant well.

Although his getting in your way is very irritating. We can ask him about it later. In the meantime, we need to talk to Lady Collins and confirm which hand Artie favoured. I don't suppose we can ask her to come to see me. She'll be in shock, no doubt.' Lady Gayle frowned and then thought better of it. She winced again but still rose from the bed. 'It's no good. I can't sleep. We can't waste the time; there's far too much to do.'

WHILE ALICE WAS TAKEN to the mortuary by one of Inspector Coward's constables, Lady Gayle made her way to the small dining room for lunch. On entering the room, she encountered Binky, Pongo, and Piffers. The three were in deep discussion at the far end of the table, and they sprang apart when they saw her enter.

'Don't mind me,' she said, wishing that she'd opened the door more slowly so she could have heard what they were discussing.

'It was nothing,' said Binky. 'Just sharing memories of poor Artie.'

'You were all at school together, I believe,' began Lady Gayle.

'Yes, we were,' said Pongo. 'How he's behaved is a dashed bad show and reflects badly on the school.'

'How so,' asked Lady Gayle, seating herself halfway down the table, directly opposite where Lord Hansen sat. She smiled at Snelling as he placed a dish of soup in front of her, and she buttered a bread roll. She looked across at Lord Hansen and tilted her head to one side.

'Because he killed himself,' replied Pongo, slowly as if explaining to a particularly dim-witted child. 'That sort of thing demonstrates what kind of men the school turns out.'

'I see,' replied Lady Gayle. She gave him a little frown as if she were considering his response. She then turned her attention to Piffers, who was intent on buttering another bread roll.

If he was aware of her gaze upon him, he gave no indication of it.

'You are sure that Artie killed himself?' she sipped the water that Snelling had poured for her, keeping her gaze on Lord Hansen.

'You were there, Lady Gayle. You saw him do it.' Pongo slammed his cutlery on the table and glared at her.

'Did I?' said Lady Gayle. She turned to face him. 'Someone clocked me on the head, Sir William. From behind. That wasn't Artie. It could not have been Artie because, as you have just said, I was sitting and watching him. Someone else hit me, and I think that someone shot Artie. I don't think he killed himself at all.'

Lord Hansen, having taken a spoonful of his soup, began to cough and gulped down his wine rapidly to clear the blockage. 'What did you say?' his eyes were as round as his open mouth.

'I said, Piffers, that I don't believe Artie killed himself. As Sir William mentioned just now, I was there. I saw everything.'

'Until you were knocked out,' said Binky. 'How are you feeling now?'

'I'll survive,' said Lady Gayle. 'Unlike Artie,' she whispered under her breath. Her eyes roved over each man at the table; one was missing. Charles Vickery, but even she could not imagine that Charles would hit her on the head, let alone kill Artie.

Just as she was thinking of him, he strolled into the dining room. He nodded at everyone present before taking a seat next to Lady Gayle. He indicated his thanks to Snelling with a dip of his head as the butler poured him some wine before turning his attention to his fellow guests.

'Have I interrupted something,' said Charles. He beckoned Snelling back to his side and whispered to him. Snelling immediately left the room. 'Were you all engaged in some juicy gossip before I walked in? Perhaps you were all talking about me?'

'Stuff and nonsense, Vickers,' replied Piffers. 'We were talking about what happened yesterday.'

Charles glanced at Lady Gayle and then returned his attention to the butler, who had returned with a dish of boiled eggs. 'I missed breakfast,' he murmured to Lady Gayle in explanation. He hit the egg smartly with the back of his spoon and began to remove the top. Golden yolk dripped down the side of the egg.

Reminded of the blood on the floor the day before, Lady Gayle had to look away, and Charles raised his eyebrows at her. 'Are you unwell, Gigi?' he said in a low voice.

She shook her head and then raised her hand to her temple, regretting the sudden movement. 'I am perfectly well,' she replied in a soft voice, glancing at the other gentlemen. They were not paying attention. 'We were talking about Artie yesterday. I said I didn't believe he had killed himself.'

'I wish you hadn't done that,' whispered Charles. 'If Artie didn't kill himself, then someone killed him, and that means they are at liberty to kill you.'

'I didn't mean to say anything. It just slipped out,' Lady Gayle hissed. Her anger at herself was transmuted into anger at Charles, and she knew she was being unfair. 'I'm sorry. I think I'm a little on edge.'

'Hardly surprising,' Charles muttered. To the others, he

said. 'What are we going to do to amuse ourselves today, chaps? Could your keeper arrange another shoot, Binky?'

Lord Ridgewell gave his guest a half smile. 'I don't think that's a terribly good idea, do you, Vickers? And in any case, the police have confiscated the shotguns for the time being.'

'Really,' replied Charles. 'What on earth for?'

'To prevent another shooting, Lord Vickery,' replied Inspector Coward as he strolled into the room.

Lady Gayle noticed Binky sit up in his chair, bristling at the inspector's impertinence. 'Thank you for clearing that up, Inspector,' he said smoothly. 'Will you take some wine perhaps or some water since we are all at lunch.'

If Inspector Coward noticed the edge to Lord Ridgewell's voice, he gave nothing away. 'Tea,' he said, nodding his thanks to the footman who brought him a cup and saucer. 'I would like to have a chat with you, Lord Ridgewell, at your earliest possible convenience, of course.'

Binky coughed and gulped his own beverage. 'After lunch,' he muttered and returned to his meal.

Silence hung over the table as the other guests ate in silence. Lady Gayle gave Charles a sideways glance, remembering the glances that Binky and he had exchanged over the dead man's body.

Charles, however, shook his head. 'Later,' he whispered.

CHAPTER TWENTY-ONE

After a much more leisurely lunch than she'd planned or even anticipated, Lady Gayle finally left the dining room. Charles was close behind her. As they crossed the hallway to the morning room, Lord Ridgewell exited the dining room with Inspector Coward close at his side, holding his lordship's elbow.

Gathering his coat from Snelling, his lordship and the police officer left St Nesban's House without a backward glance.

Lady Gayle whirled around to protest but was quelled by a glare from the inspector. 'Oh my goodness, Inspector Coward,' she exclaimed. 'You're arresting the wrong man.'

'I have my reasons,' said the inspector. 'This way, your lordship.'

Lady Gayle dashed towards the stairs and ran up them as quickly as she could. Lord Vickery, on the other hand, darted after the inspector and Lord Ridgewell. She could hear him calling for his car to be brought round.

She raced to Bundle's room and banged loudly on the door, not waiting for an answer before she burst into the room.

Bundle was once again on her chaise lounge sipping tea. 'What on earth?' she said at Lady Gayle's hurried entrance.

'It's Binky,' cried Lady Gayle. 'I'm really sorry, Bundle, there's no easy way to tell you this, but the blighter has only gone and arrested Binky.'

'Blighter?' said Bundle. 'Which blighter are you talking about?'

'The inspector,' replied Lady Gayle. 'He's got this all wrong. He's making a huge mistake. Binky didn't do this terrible thing.'

The cup slipped from Bundle's grasp, and Mary stepped in quickly to prevent the tea from spilling everywhere.

'But Binky's innocent,' said Bundle. Her voice was barely audible; her face drained of all colour.

'I know,' replied Lady Gayle. 'I can't understand what the inspector's doing.'

'You must find out who did, Gigi,' demanded Bundle. She rested her hands on her huge stomach. 'He can't leave me alone in this state. If he's found guilty...'

She said no more, and neither did Lady Gayle. If Binky was found guilty of murder, then he would pay the ultimate price.

'I promise you, it won't come to that,' replied Lady Gayle. She paced the room for a moment, and then, when Mary made her realise that she was not improving things for poor Bundle, she said, 'I will find out who did this. I promise you.' Lady Gayle marched out of the room, but once in the corridor, she leaned against the wall, wondering how she was ever going to make sense of what had happened.

Hearing voices whispering on the main stairs, Lady Gayle made her way towards the spot in the minstrels' gallery where she'd secreted herself only a few days beforehand to peek over the balcony. A man and woman were running downstairs. Lady Gayle decided to follow them.

They took the same side door Lady Gayle had used on New Year's Day, but instead of going into the garden, they ducked into the orangery. Lady Gayle gave them a few seconds before pushing down the handle and easing the door open.

Their voices were low and hurried, and she crept closer to hear more.

'Are you sure?' the man hissed.

'Yes,' the woman's low voice caught on a sob. 'I went to his room so that we could walk down to dinner together. He likes that, says it makes us look more like a happily married couple.'

The man's laugh was harsh. 'What a joke,' he said.

'I know, but I can't let his—his—proclivities become public knowledge.'

'I understand, but at least he won't hang nowadays.'

'No, fortunately, that's not the punishment any longer, but he would still be jailed. With hard labour, Willie. While I don't love him as a wife should, I couldn't do that to him.'

'You are such a darling woman, Lizzie. But surely you would have grounds to divorce him.'

'I have already spoken with a solicitor and, sadly no, divorce is not an option.' The lady's voice broke. 'I would need to provide evidence of an affair. That would mean employing a private investigator to take photographs. The photographs would be in all the papers, Willie. The shame would break Edward and me too.'

There was silence for a moment, and the lady spoke again. 'Then there's Ascot, Willie. If I divorced him, even if I could avoid the public shame, I'd never be allowed in the Royal Enclosure ever again.'

'Well, if Ascot is what's most important to you, then we're stuck, aren't we?' replied the man with a bitter voice. 'It's good to know where your priorities lie, Lizzie.'

Lady Gayle felt she'd listened long enough, especially now she knew exactly who the couple were. She edged away from the potted palm, her chiffon catching on the greenery and causing her to utter a curse.

'Who's there?' called the man.

'It's me,' called Lady Gayle.

Sir William Greenwood and Lady Elizabeth Hansen sprang apart.

'Don't mind me,' said Lady Gayle. 'I was hoping to talk to you both, and now I can. Two birds with one stone. Or something like that.'

'It's not how it looks,' burst out Lizzie Hansen.

'Oh, Lizzie,' murmured Lady Gayle. 'It's exactly what it looks like and more to the point, everyone knows, but I do need to talk to Pongo about the day of the shooting.'

'You do?' replied Sir William. He tilted his head, a guarded expression on his face.

'You left early.' Lady Gayle made it a statement rather than a question, and Pongo nodded.

'I had agreed to meet Lizzie while Piffers was busy with the shoot. I'd opted not to have the under-keeper load for me so I could slip off without anyone noticing.'

'Did Artie leave at the same time?'

'Artie?' Pongo frowned. 'I don't know. I saw him arguing with Piffers when we broke for a hot toddy and soup. I didn't see him after that.'

'What were they arguing about?' said Lady Gayle, deciding that she needed to talk with Lord Hansen as soon as possible.

Pongo shrugged. 'No idea, I didn't realise they had anything to discuss, let alone argue about. I would have stayed to find out more, but I wanted to be with Lizzie.' He took her hands in his, and they gazed deeply into each other's eyes.

Lady Gayle coughed, and they jumped apart again. 'I really do need you two to concentrate. Binky has been arrested.'

'For what?' Pongo pushed Lizzie Hansen behind him as if he could protect her from arrest.

'I think for Artie's murder,' Lady Gayle said. 'He has a perfect alibi for the other murder.'

'Artie didn't kill himself?' Lizzie Hansen peeked around Pongo's shoulder. 'Are you sure?'

'As sure as I can be. Why? What do you know?'

'We didn't see anything,' protested Pongo.

'That's not quite true, is it, Willie?' said Lady Hansen.

Lady Gayle bit the inside of her lip, struggling not to laugh at the expression on Pongo's face each time he was called Willie. *Clearly, he hates it. Why doesn't he say something?* She turned to Lady Hansen. 'What did you see?'

Lady Hansen took a deep breath, 'Well,' she said, exhaling, 'yesterday I went to see Edward so that we could walk down to the drawing room together. He was in his dressing room, and he was washing his hands.'

'I see,' said Lady Gayle, although she was struggling to see the point.

'You don't understand,' said Lizzie. 'When he dried his hands, there was blood on the towel. He told me he'd cut himself, but there was no wound that I could see. He told me not to make a fuss, and so I didn't. He could get very angry at times. When he did—'

'You don't have to tell her that,' said Sir William, placing a protective arm around her shoulders.

Lizzie patted his hand. 'I do,' she said. 'I want to tell her everything. I am sick of secrets. When Edward was angry, he would lash out. He wasn't often angry, but I had learned to keep my distance when he was.

'So, when I saw the blood, and he refused to talk about it, I didn't ask anything more. We went down to dinner as if nothing had happened. That's when we found out that Artie had killed himself.'

'And now? Where do you think the blood came from now?'

'I have been wondering if Edward shot Artie. I didn't know that they had argued, but I know Edward was upset by something on New Year's Eve. He was very out of sorts that evening.'

Lady Gayle thought back. Not knowing Lord Hansen well, she had taken his ill humour as simply his normal mode of behaviour.

'Do you know what upset him on New Year's Eve, Lady Hansen?'

'I can answer that,' said Sir William. 'Jack Parsons turning up here. I saw Piffers with him in the early afternoon. Not long after lunch. We were walking up to the shoot, and I happened to look behind and see Piffers shouting at the man.'

'You didn't think to say so before?' Lady Gayle thought back to the glance she'd seen between Binky and Charles.

Had they also seen Lord Hansen arguing with the dead man and chosen to keep quiet?

'Look, Parsons was a brute,' hissed Sir William. 'I was surprised, shocked even to see Parsons here, but I'm not a gambler, and so I had nothing to worry about.'

'Was Lord Hansen a gambler?' said Lady Gayle.

Sir William shook his head. 'He liked a flutter, but I don't think he had large debts. But Parsons wasn't above making a bit of money on the side.'

'How so?' asked Lady Gayle.

Sir William and Lady Hansen exchanged worried glances, and then she pressed her lips together and nodded her assent.

'Piffers had once been—I suppose *friendly* is the best term to use—with Parsons,' said Sir William. 'Ever since then, Piffers has been paying him for his silence.'

CHAPTER TWENTY-TWO

'Blackmail,' whispered Lady Gayle. 'Do you know how long it had been going on?'

Sir William shrugged, 'It's not something we really discussed,' he said. 'Since I'm, well, you can see the tricky spot I'm in.'

Lady Gayle nodded. Pongo was in an awkward position as the lover of his friend's wife. Whilst Lord Hansen had no physical interest in his wife, no man wanted to be widely known as a cuckold. There was also the danger that if Lord Hansen's inclinations were widely known, he could be jailed or receive a heavy fine. 'Any ideas,' she repeated. 'How long ago did their affair start?'

'About a year,' interrupted Lady Hansen. 'My husband and I may not be close, but I occasionally overhear things. I believe Parsons came to visit the London house on a regular basis. My sister and my niece were staying with us for the Season. We came back early one day from a simply ghastly party, and Edward was—entertaining.'

'Lizzie, you didn't tell me any of this?' Pongo clutched

her hands, holding them to his lips and covering them in kisses.

She pulled away gently. 'What could I say,' she said. 'Fortunately, my sister still doesn't know, and my niece is far too innocent to understand what she saw.'

'What *did* she see?'

Lizzie Hansen flushed. 'I'd rather not say,' she said, her gaze fixed on the tiled floor. 'But it was awful. Edward and I had a terrible argument, and he agreed not to have anyone back at the house ever again. He told me later that the man had cut up rough, but he said a few guineas had smoothed things over.' She shook her head. 'Edward always believed that money was the best policy. I should have realised that when paying a man like that, once would not be enough.'

'You weren't to know,' said Lady Gayle. 'One payment should have been sufficient, but it never is.'

Turning to Sir William, she said, 'Let me get this straight... you saw Parsons and Piffers arguing on New Year's Eve, but Piffers can prove he was nowhere near the man when he was shot.'

They both nodded. 'But then you saw blood on Lord Hansen's towel in his room yesterday?' said Lady Gayle.

Lizzie Hansen nodded. 'Yes,' she whispered anxiously. 'But what does that prove?'

'I'm not sure yet,' said Lady Gayle. 'I do hope that it proves the inspector has it wrong though, and that Binky cannot possibly have shot Artie. I must talk to the inspector at once.'

LADY GAYLE HURRIED towards the orangery door and out into the corridor. She needed to talk to the inspector urgently.

Calling for Snelling, Lady Gayle asked him to have her

car brought around to the front of the house while she readied herself for the drive into the village.

Once dressed in her heavy coat and her thick socks and boots, Lady Gayle felt ready for the challenge. Just as she was on the point of leaving the house, Bundle's maid, Mary, came running down the stairs. She skidded to a halt when Snelling raised his eyebrows at her, but the urgency of her errand overcame her surprise at the butler's shock at her impropriety. She broke into a run again.

'Lady Gayle, Lady Gayle,' she panted. 'I'm glad I caught you. Lady Ridgewell needs you. She says the baby's coming.'

'It can't be,' replied Lady Gayle. 'It's far too early. There's a month to go at least, isn't there?'

'Yes, my lady,' puffed Mary. 'I think it's the shock of Lord Ridgewell's arrest that's brought it on. Will you come, my lady? Oh please, will you come?'

Lady Gayle raised her eyes heavenward. 'What about the midwife?' she asked. 'Can we bring her here?'

'No, my lady, she went to stay with family in Derby for Christmas and New Year since the baby wasn't expected for another month.' Mary clutched her heaving chest, her face creased in panic.

'This is exactly what I was afraid of,' Lady Gayle said. 'Has Alice returned?'

'She's taking a cup of tea in the kitchen, my lady,' said Snelling.

'Oh good,' replied Lady Gayle. 'Snelling, could you let her know what's happening and also arrange for Lord Ridgewell's car to be made ready? I don't think we'll get Lady Ridgewell in the Austin.'

'Very good, my lady,' said Snelling, as unflappable as

ever. He headed towards the doorway which led to the kitchen, and Lady Gayle raced upstairs.

Panting, she burst into Bundle's room without knocking. Bundle was padding back and forth in front of the fire, head bowed and sweating profusely. She had one hand on her swollen belly and was trying to rub her own back with the other. 'I think it's time,' she said on seeing Lady Gayle. 'I don't know why you're looking so scared. All you've got to do is drive.'

'Snelling is getting someone to bring the car around. Can you make it downstairs, or do you need someone to carry you?'

Bundle stared at her. 'I'd rather trundle down under my own steam,' she said. 'If someone tries to lift me, there's a good chance they'll drop me. Blast that husband of mine. He's supposed to be here.'

'I'll ask Pongo to drive the Austin to the police station. He'll find Charles, and they can see if the inspector will let Binky go.'

Bundle grabbed Lady Gayle's forearm, digging her nails in deep. It was all Lady Gayle could do not to scream out loud. 'He's not guilty, is he?' Bundle hissed. 'Tell me he's not guilty?'

Lady Gayle prised Bundle's nails from her flesh. 'I don't believe he is,' she said, rubbing at the half-moons indented on her forearm. 'I was just on the point of going to talk to the inspector when Mary caught me. It was lucky she did. Another couple of minutes and I would have gone.'

Bundle moaned and went pale. Mary held her hand and threw a blanket around her mistress' shoulders. 'Come along, my lady,' she said. 'Let's get you to the hospital.'

Bundle nodded feverishly, and Lady Gayle followed them down the stairs and across the hallway. Outside,

Binky's car was waiting with the engine running. Landers, the St Nesban's chauffeur, hobbled around the front of the car to help Lady Ridgewell onto the back seat. 'Landers,' she said. 'I do hope you've not been driving with that broken ankle.'

'Only from the stables, milady,' he said. 'No further than that.' Despite his bandaged ankle, he made sure she was settled in the back of the car.

Mary got in beside her mistress. Lady Gayle and Alice leapt into the front seats. She put the car into gear, and it lurched forward. Biting her lip at the sheer power of the engine, she tried to apply the accelerator more gently. The engine responded with a purr and with a shower of gravel over the onlookers as the large car and its precious cargo rattled away down the drive.

It was nearly twenty miles to the cottage hospital, and Lady Gayle hoped fervently that her friend's baby was prepared to be patient.

CHAPTER TWENTY-THREE

KEEPING HER ATTENTION ON THE ROAD AHEAD, LADY GAYLE HOPED that Pongo would be able to find Charles. She was confident that together, the two men could persuade Inspector Coward to allow Lord Ridgewell to be close at hand for his wife during the birth of their child. She gripped the steering wheel, her knuckles whitening. Low winter sun peeked over the hedgerows, hitting her full in the face. Its brightness obscured the icy patches on the roads, although she was alert to the danger. Snow had not been forecast, but the sub-zero temperatures overnight rendered the roads lethal. She hoped that Pongo was able to drive safely.

At a groan from Bundle, she pressed her foot to the accelerator, and the car nosed forward, eating up the distance. She reached forward to wipe the condensation on the windscreen away with her hands. It only made matters worse. From the passenger seat, she snatched up the glove that Alice offered her to wipe the screen. It improved things, but only slightly. She opened the window a crack to allow some of the warmth from their combined breathing and body heat to escape.

Her mind still raced, going over the clues and information that she had. Suspects, she thought. Artie was the best suspect for killing Parsons; even though he had no reason to do so, he had both the means and the opportunity. But did that make him a killer? She shook her head.

Lord Hansen had good reason to kill Parsons, but although he had the means, he had alibis, placing him well away from the victim. What did he and Artie argue about? What did they *have* to argue about? Lady Gayle thought back to New Year's Eve and the card game. Piffers had called Artie a coward. *Was* he really on the cusp of telling the whole world about Artie's secret?

'No, that can't be it,' she muttered. Artie would then reveal Lord Hansen's dark secret. Even as she had the thought, she dismissed it. Artie Collins would have carried that secret to the grave, and he had.

What about Binky, though? Dear, sweet Binky. Lady Gayle could not imagine him killing anyone. She knew from their earlier conversation that he tried to avoid killing the pheasants even though he was happy enough to provide the opportunity for his friends. She remembered him telling her that he held the opinion that it was very unsporting to shoot an unarmed opponent. Had Parsons been armed? But no, Binky had his gamekeeper with him all afternoon. He had no time to shoot anyone, let alone disrobe them and place them in a bonfire.

And that's another thing, she thought. Why remove the garments? Why not burn them with the victim? Removing them made no sense at all unless—unless they had a value on their own? But what?

Bundle moaned again, and Lady Gayle snatched a look at her friend's pale face. It brought back other memories. Blinking tears away, she clenched her jaw. Concentrate, she told herself. Don't think about that now. But unbidden and uninvited, the thoughts intruded. A nurse mopping her head; Sister Edwards commanding her to relax and let them do their work. Then the blood, the coppery smell, filling her nostrils and making her gag. Lady Gayle wiped her eyes and then the windscreen. *Concentrate,* she muttered. *You have to get Bundle to the hospital. Don't mess this up.*

'Alice,' she said. 'When you saw Parsons in the corridor outside Lady Ridgewell's door, was he standing still, or was he walking?'

'Walking towards me, milady,' confirmed Alice with a quick peek to the back seat to ensure no one was paying any attention to their conversation.

Lady Gayle pursed her lips. 'I wonder if he was just walking past the door when you saw him?' she said. 'He could have left another room and be heading toward the stairs.'

'That's as maybe, milady, but if that's the case, he would have come from Mrs Bishop's bedroom. What would an old woman like her want with a young man?'

Lady Gayle flicked one eyebrow upwards. Mrs Bishop was only in middle years, and Mr Parsons was a very well-built young man. Not unattractive in his own way, but of course, he batted for the other team, she reminded herself. 'I'm sure I don't know,' she said with a smile. 'Perhaps he worked for her.' As she said it, an idea wormed its way into her head. Why *had* Mrs Bishop been invited to St Nesbans? The lady had seemed out of place most of the time. She was older than the rest of the party; she wasn't of the same social class, but she was rich. She was very rich indeed. Perhaps that's why she was invited. Bundle was breathing more quietly now, so she risked the question. 'Bundle, what do you know about Mrs Bishop?'

'Who?' grunted Bundle. 'Why on earth do you want to talk about *her*? I do have other things on my mind right now.'

'I know, but she doesn't really fit in, and I wondered why she was there.'

'You'll have to ask Binky. He invited her. Business, he said and—' Bundle's voice broke off as another contraction seized her body.

'I know it's not much further, my lady,' cried Mary. 'But I don't know how much longer Lady Ridgewell can wait.'

'I'm sure it won't be too long,' said Lady Gayle, although, in truth, she had no idea. The cottage hospital was new, built in commemoration of the men who had died in the Great War, or so she had been told, and she was uncertain of its exact location.

'Turn here, my lady,' called Mary. She had pulled herself forward and was clinging on to the front seats so she could take a look at the road. 'I asked Landers to bring me here so we'd know exactly where it was.'

'Well done,' said Lady Gayle through gritted teeth. She fought the steering wheel on the icy road and turned where Mary had indicated. The car crept up a narrow road, bordered on each side with low stone walls. Soon, the road opened out, and she swept into an area in front of the hospital itself. Alice leapt out of the car and ran inside, calling for a doctor. Lady Gayle opened the rear door for Mary and Lady Ridgewell just as a nurse and a man in a white coat ran from the building with a wheelchair.

Bundle was bundled into the wheelchair and rushed away. Lady Gayle leaned against the car. 'Well, that was quite something,' she said.

'How are you, milady?' said Alice.

Lady Gayle brushed the question aside. 'Perfectly fine,' she said, staring at the plaque over the golden stone which comprised the hospital entrance. 'I'm absolutely peachy.'

As Lady Gayle began making her way towards the doorway, a black car with a clanging bell rushed into the car park. Binky leapt out, closely followed by Inspector Coward and PC Kennard. Binky raced past her to the hospital reception. Lady Gayle saw him dash towards the corridor indicated by the nurse, and she waited for the police officers to join her.

'Is he still under arrest?' she said, facing the two men with her arms folded.

'I needed to talk to him,' replied Inspector Coward. 'I still need to talk to him. Events got away from us, but far be it for me to get between a man and his child.'

'You'll be between them if you hang him for murder,' said Lady Gayle.

'That's outside of my responsibility,' replied the inspector. 'My job is to find the evidence and present it to the court.'

'You have no evidence, Inspector,' replied Lady Gayle. 'Lord Ridgewell cannot have killed Jack Parsons, and he has no reason to kill Lord Collins. I rather think that you are searching in the wrong places for your killer.

'Now, if you'll excuse me. I would like to spend some time with my friends.' Turning swiftly, Lady Gayle marched into the hospital, closely followed by Alice. She left the inspector and police constable behind in her wake.

CHAPTER TWENTY-FOUR

Binky was pacing in the small waiting room when she entered. They were alone, and Lady Gayle thought it was as good a place to talk as any. Alice said she would see what she could do about finding them all a nice cup of tea.

'Please sit down, Binky,' said Lady Gayle. 'I'm nervous enough without you pacing.'

'Dash it all, Gigi,' said Lord Ridgewell. He plonked himself on a wooden chair next to her. 'The baby isn't due for another month. I blame the police for this. If they hadn't arrested me—'

'Are you truly under arrest for murder?' said Lady Gayle.

'Not as such,' replied Binky. He rose and began to pace again. 'They had several questions for me, and the inspector thought that it was better if I answered them at the station.'

'What sort of questions?'

'About my connections with Parsons and my connections with The 43 Club.' Binky plunged his hands into his pockets and began patting his jacket. He discovered his cigarette case in his breast pocket, but a lighter eluded him.

Lady Gayle offered him a box of matches that must have been left on the window ledge by another anxious father.

When he'd lit the cigarette, Binky inhaled deeply and then blew the smoke out towards the light fitting. 'They also wanted to know about my relationship with Mrs Bishop.'

Lady Gayle opened her mouth, but no words came.

Binky laughed. 'Not that kind of relationship, you dope,' he said. 'They wanted to know why I had invited her to stay over Christmas.'

Lady Gayle remained silent, although she arched an eyebrow at him. It was the very question she had for him herself.

'I suppose everyone wants to know that,' he said. He finished the cigarette and lit a second one from the stub of the first.

'You would not be wrong,' said Lady Gayle. She didn't mention quite how desperate she was to know too. Just let him talk, she thought.

'Mrs Bishop is another regular at The 43 Club,' said Binky after a moment. He stared at the glowing end of the cigarette.

'Does she have many gambling debts?' Lady Gayle said, unable to stop herself from interrupting.

Binky frowned at her and shook his head. 'She doesn't gamble. She likes to watch other people gamble.'

Lady Gayle thought back to New Year's Eve. Mrs Bishop had hovered on the edge of the card game. No one had invited her to join in—something she'd not given much consideration to at the time.

'Isn't that a little odd?' she said. 'Where's the fun it that?'

'Apparently, you'd be surprised,' replied Binky. His eyes snapped towards the door as it opened.

A young nurse stood in the doorway. She waved her hand in front of her face to disperse the smoke. 'Lord Ridgewell,' she said. 'You have a little girl. Mother and baby are both well. Would you like to come and meet your daughter?'

Binky whirled around, 'Oh gosh, would I?' he said, giving Lady Gayle a peck on the cheek before he dashed away. When Alice returned with a tray and three cups of tea, Lady Gayle was alone.

'It's a girl,' she said and burst into tears.

If Inspector Coward was surprised when he entered the waiting room and saw her ladyship's reddened eyes, he said nothing about it.

'Why don't you go back to the house,' he said. 'I'm told Lord Ridgewell will be here for quite some time. And Sir William has offered to remain to drive him back.'

'You're releasing Binky?' asked Lady Gayle.

'He was never under arrest,' said the inspector. 'I wanted to see if someone showed their hand if I took his lordship away. With the baby making her entrance, my ruse has been rather overshadowed.'

'You arrested him under false pretences,' said Lady Gayle, placing her hands on her hips.

'Not at all,' replied the inspector. 'I explained the situation to his lordship, and he agreed to play along. We didn't expect it to have such an impact on her ladyship.' He bowed his head. 'I suppose that's a lesson for all of us.'

'Indeed,' retorted Lady Gayle. 'Come along, Alice. I think we have better things to do.' Finding herself absolutely furious with the inspector, she stalked out of the room; head held high to keep more tears from forming. Once out of the inspector's sight, she dabbed her eyes with a handkerchief that Alice produced for her.

'Are you safe to drive, milady,' said Alice.

'I'll be fine. We'll just take it nice and slowly.'

'Oh good,' replied Alice. 'That *will* make a pleasant change.'

Lady Gayle and Alice drove in silence for several minutes, both lost in their own thoughts.

'We need to work out what's going on, Alice,' said Lady Gayle after a few miles. 'Lady Ridgewell can't bring her baby home with a murderer on the loose, can she?'

'No, milady,' said Alice. 'Who do you think did it?'

Lady Gayle was silent for a moment. 'Well, Lord Ridgewell is in the clear, isn't he?' she said finally. 'He wasn't keen on the pheasant shoot. He told me he'd done enough shooting during the war to want to do any more now. Like the card game, he only organised it to entertain the gentlemen.'

'What about Lord Collins, milady?'

'Perhaps,' said Lady Gayle. 'He doesn't have a good alibi for the afternoon. He didn't have someone to load his gun for him, so there's no one to vouch for where he was.'

'But Sir William didn't have a loader either, did he?' Alice replied.

'Oh gosh, of course, you're right. I thought he was sharing with Charles, but that was Piffers. However, Pongo does have an alibi. He was with Lady Hansen.'

'It has been whispered about below stairs, milady,' said Alice. 'Only in the most discreet of terms you understand.'

'Of course, nothing gets missed by staff, does it? What's the thinking with the other servants, Alice? Who do they have their money on?'

'Lord Hansen or perhaps Lord Vickery, milady,' replied Alice. 'Since Lord Collins has killed himself, everyone thinks it's highly likely to be him, isn't it? They believe he did it out of guilt.'

Lady Gayle sighed deeply. 'Yes, Alice. I agree, *if* Artie did kill himself, then it's extremely likely he's responsible for the death of Jack Parsons.'

'*If*, milady?' Alice and Lady Gayle exchanged glances.

'Yes, Alice. If he killed himself.' Lady Gayle stared out at the road ahead, pursing her lips. 'I forgot in all the excitement. Was the young man you saw in the corridor the same man who was shot?'

'It was milady,' replied Alice. 'But I still can't fathom what he was doing with Mrs Bishop if it was her room he'd been to.'

'Perhaps he had worked for her?' mused Lady Gayle.

'Doing what, milady?' said Alice. 'Oh, you don't mean as a... I can't think of the word.'

'A gigolo, Alice?' replied Lady Gayle. 'No, I don't think so. Jackie Parsons' preferences ran in quite a different direction. We know he was working for the gangster William Saffron. I'm still struggling to see where Mrs Bishop fits in. Does she owe money? She was a regular at The 43 Club as well.'

'I thought she was rich,' sniffed Alice. 'Why would she owe anything to a gangster?'

'I don't know, Alice. Binky is rich, and he owes a gangster lots of money. But then Mrs Bishop didn't gamble. Forgive me. I'm rather thinking aloud. Throwing ideas into the air and seeing where they land.'

'Well, if that's what we're doing, milady,' said Alice. 'Could Mrs Bishop have killed Jack Parsons? After all, it's not the first time we've found out how wicked some ladies can be, is it?'

'No, Alice, you're quite right, it isn't,' said Lady Gayle.

CHAPTER
TWENTY-FIVE

When Lady Gayle arrived at St Nesban's House, news from the hospital had reached Snelling by telephone. 'His lordship asked me to serve champagne as soon as you arrived, my lady,' he said. 'All the other guests are gathered in the drawing room.'

'Do they know?' asked Lady Gayle.

Snelling gave the merest indication of the negative. 'He wanted you to make the announcement since, he says, that without you, the baby would have been born without any medical help at all.'

'Thank you, Snelling,' said Lady Gayle.

'Her young ladyship is to be called Sylvia, my lady. After Lady Redmond-Smythe,' said Snelling. 'Lord Ridgewell said he was more than happy for you to tell his guests.'

'Sylvia?' said Lady Gayle. 'Oh my.' She crumpled and collapsed onto a hallway chair.

Snelling produced a large white handkerchief seemingly from nowhere and offered it to her. 'Would my lady like a moment to compose herself?'

Lady Gayle blew her nose and stuffed the handkerchief in the pocket of her winter coat. 'No, thank you, Snelling,' she said. 'These are happy tears, and I think they are acceptable.' She shrugged out of her coat and gave it to the butler.

'Very good, my lady,' replied Snelling with a small bow. He laid the coat on a hall chair and snapped his fingers. Two footmen appeared with trays filled with glasses and bottles in ice buckets. 'If your ladyship would follow me?'

Snelling opened the drawing room door, and Lady Gayle strolled in. Everyone's head whirled to face her.

'It's a girl,' she said. She held onto the upright of a sofa, begging her knees not to give way. 'Her name is going to be Sylvia.'

For a moment, there was a hush as those gathered took in the child's name. Lady Gayle jumped as champagne corks popped. She accepted a glass of the delicious bubbles from Snelling's tray. When she caught his eye, she spotted that they were glistening as much as her own surely were.

EXHAUSTED from the excitement of the day and the revelations, Lady Gayle sidled towards the drawing room door. She stepped into the hallway with a sigh of relief. The emotions of the day had worn her out, and she needed to take a bath and relax. Scarcely had she placed one foot on the carpeted stair than someone called her name. She turned, surprised to see who had spoken.

'Lady Collins,' she said. 'What might I do for you?'

'Could we talk?' Pamela Collins' dark eyes were underlined with darker shadows. She looked as if she hadn't slept in weeks.

'Of course,' replied Lady Gayle, 'perhaps you'd like to come to my room?'

Lady Collins nodded, and they wandered up the stairs in silence. When Lady Gayle opened her door, Alice was in the adjoining room with her sewing. She nodded at her mistress and left immediately, leaving the two ladies with some privacy.

'Won't you take a seat,' said Lady Gayle, indicating the two armchairs by the cheerful-looking fire.

'Thank you.' Lady Collins smoothed out her skirt and sat in silence, her hands clasped together in her lap.

Lady Gayle sat opposite her and mirrored the pose. After sitting in silence for a while, impatience overcame her. 'What did you want to talk about, Lady Collins?'

'Call me Pamela,' replied Lady Collins. She gazed into the fire, still reluctant to speak, twisting her hands together. The silence grew heavy as Lady Collins still said nothing.

'Pamela, we're completely alone now. What is worrying you so much? I can see you're not sleeping.'

'Is it any wonder?' sighed Pamela. 'I think, no, I *know* that my husband was murdered, and I know who did it.'

'Tell me,' urged Lady Gayle. 'Tell me, do you know who did this heinous thing to poor Artie? Did they murder Jack Parsons too?'

'Who?' said Pamela Collins, her face screwed up in confusion.

'The young man whose body we found on New Year's Eve.'

'Oh, him. No, I know for a fact Artie killed him.'

Lady Gayle felt her jaw slacken slightly. Alice and the staff were right. Although she had her suspicions about

Artie, she'd still struggled to come up with a motive. 'Do you know why?'

'Piffers made him.' Pamela Collins shrugged. She looked around the room. 'Do you have anything to drink here? I could do with a snifter.'

Frowning, Lady Gayle cast her eyes around the room. Of course, the dressing table drawer. She shot across the room and collected the bottle of brandy that Alice had placed there for her. There was only one brandy glass, which she gave to Pamela Collins. She passed a large brandy to her guest, who raised the glass to her lips and took a gulp. With her own brandy, she could only find a tooth mug to drink from. Gosh, I must make sure I keep a better brand in my room, she thought after taking a small sip and grimacing. She placed the tooth mug to one side before dragging herself back to the matter in hand.

'Why would Piffers make Artie do that?' she asked, even though she had half an idea. 'How *could* he make Artie kill someone?' She had an even better idea about that, but she wanted someone to confirm her suspicions.

'Piffers had something over Artie. Something that no one else knew about.'

'Artie told me that he was a coward.' When Pamela Collins shot a venomous glare at her, Lady Gayle wished she'd kept her mouth shut.

'Artie was an absolute darling,' Lady Collins said, taking another sip of her drink. 'The sweetest man, but he could be such an idiot. He wasn't a coward, but he had suffered terribly. Dreadful things happened to him during the war. You would not believe how he suffered. He was going to be executed as a coward, and his father paid someone off to release him. In the end, that turned out to be the worst thing the old lord could have done.'

'Who was paid off?'

'Lord Hansen. He took the money and squirrelled Artie away from the barracks. Artie has been terrified of him ever since. Every time he's wanted to make a clean breast of it, that blasted Piffers threatened him.'

'But if Artie wanted to come clean, how could Lord Hansen still threaten him? Surely taking the money makes Piffers equally guilty.'

'Piffers was violent. He threatened to kill Artie if he told anyone. One night, I found Artie in his bedroom at our London house. Artie was in a terrible way. Piffers, or maybe that friend of his, had used poor Artie as a punching bag. Artie had a black eye and several broken ribs. He was terrified. If he had killed himself then, I would not have blamed him, but he didn't, and I cannot believe that he would have done so now.' She laid her hand on her tummy, and Lady Gayle's own stomach lurched.

'You're pregnant,' she whispered.

Pamela Collins nodded. 'Artie was so happy, but he wanted Piffers off his back, so he agreed to do one last thing to make things square, but then he couldn't live with what he had done.'

'He was playing with his service revolver when I saw him in the cellar.' Lady Gayle could not help herself. Even though she didn't think Artie would go through with it, there was no doubt that death had been on his mind.

'He was meeting Piffers. I think he wanted to have it out with him. He took the gun for protection; just in case, you know.'

Lady Gayle nodded, then one final thought occurred. 'Which hand did Artie favour, say, for writing letters.'

Pamela Collins gave a faint smile. 'Oh, poor Artie. It caused him so many problems when he was a boy. His governess said using the left hand was evil. Something to do with the devil, so she tied it up when he did his lessons. She was sacked when his father found out. Artie was left-handed. Always has been.'

CHAPTER TWENTY-SIX

'We have to tell the inspector,' Lady Gayle said. She pulled Lady Collins to her feet. 'We have to find him now and tell him to release Binky.'

Despite the inspector telling her that he had taken Lord Ridgewell away to flush out the real killer, she wasn't sure how he could have been so misguided. Convinced that Binky could not have killed Artie, Lady Gayle was now certain she was in possession of the truth. She knew the real killer was completely ruthless and would never make the mistake of giving themselves away. 'Come along, Pamela,' she said. 'You must hurry.'

Pamela Collins swayed and collapsed back in the armchair. 'I'm so sleepy,' she said. 'I think I'd like to rest here, just for a few moments longer.'

'I don't think we have time to rest. We need to find the inspector.' Lady Gayle tugged at Pamela's hand to pull her from the chair, but Lady Collins really had fallen asleep.

'How infuriating,' muttered Lady Gayle. She was on the point of dashing out of the room and leaving Lady Collins to sleep when she stopped. She placed her hands on her hips and frowned. Why the sudden change in demeanour, she thought. Lady Collins had been eager to talk to her and alert throughout the entire conversation. What's changed, she wondered.

Leaning over her guest, she removed the brandy glass from Lady Collins' limp hand. Pamela's skin was hot to the touch, and Lady Gayle reached for the pulse in her wrist. It was racing.

'Oh no, what have you eaten?' But even as she said the words, Lady Gayle realised that it wasn't food but drink which had impacted her guest. She glanced at the brandy in the tooth mug that she had left untouched after her one small sip. She muttered a curse under her breath and raised the glass to her lips. She stuck the tip of her tongue in the liquid. It tasted slightly unusual, but the smell was definitely off. Since when did brandy smell like bitter almonds?

Leaving Lady Collins by the fire, Lady Gayle ran into the corridor, calling for help. Alice came at once, followed by Snelling. 'We need something to make Lady Collins vomit,' she said.

'An emetic, my lady?' said Snelling. 'At once.' He called Mrs Weatherly on the house telephone and gave his orders. When the foul-smelling concoction arrived, Lady Gayle sat with Lady Collins, forcing her to drink it. Alice rushed into the room, 'The doctor is on his way,' she said.

'Good,' said Lady Gayle 'I just hope he's not too late.' As she spoke, Inspector Coward rushed into her bedroom, and the room became just that little bit smaller. Allowing Alice and Snelling to take over, she edged into the corridor. Inspector Coward followed.

'I think it may have been meant for me,' Lady Gayle gasped. 'It was in my brandy. I always used to keep a bottle to one side for emergencies. An old habit from my ambulance days when I couldn't sleep.'

If the inspector had views on medicinal brandy, he kept them to himself, but he did raise an eyebrow. 'Who knew about it?' he said.

'My maid. I don't think anyone else. Why would anyone want to kill me?'

'Because you'd got too close to the truth,' replied the inspector. 'How often do you have a quiet tipple on your own?'

Not very often. I had one after we'd found the body. The first body, that is,' she said. 'Just for the shock. Mr Snelling sent me a bottle of brandy up with one of the footmen.'

'So, it's likely that the entire household knew. The servants and possibly their employers too.'

'Oh dear, that means if it *is* poisoned, then anyone in the household could have sneaked in.'

That's possible, certainly.' Inspector Coward scratched his head. 'Give me the rest of it. I'll get it tested.'

'Where's Binky,' Lady Gayle said, changing the subject away from someone trying to kill her.

'He's at the hospital with his family. I think that's the safest place for him just now. Did Lady Collins have anything interesting to say?'

'Yes,' said Lady Gayle. 'Artie was definitely left-handed, so he would not have shot himself with his right hand. She also said that Piffers, I mean Lord Hansen, was blackmailing Artie and made him kill Jack Parsons.

'You do agree that Lord Hansen killed Artie, don't you?' said Lady Gayle.

'Yes, I do now,' replied Inspector Coward. 'I'm not so sure about the poison though. That's more of a woman's weapon.'

Lady Gayle folded her arms. 'Is it, Inspector? Always?'

'Well, there are many reasons to use poison,' said the inspector, his face glowing. 'It's just that it tends to be used by the weaker sex much more often.'

'The weaker sex?' repeated Lady Gayle in a soft voice. 'Even after everything women did during the war, you still believe that we are weaker than men?'

'No. Yes. Well, no, not really.' The inspector was flustered and edged away, or he would have if he'd not been hard against the wall.

'Which is it, Inspector? Women are weaker than men, or they are not?'

Inspector Coward twisted his trilby around in his hands. 'Perhaps this is a conversation for another time,' he said. 'I still have a killer to catch.'

'Yes, *we* do, don't we?' said Lady Gayle.

THE INSPECTOR SCURRIED towards the top of the stairs and sprinted down them. Lady Gayle heard him calling for his constables as he ran. She decided to leave finding Lord Hansen to him. After checking that Lady Collins was in the doctor's good hands, she decided to clear up something else that had been bothering her.

Calling Gaspod to her side, Lady Gayle strode out the side exit of St Nesban's House. For a long time, she had been confused as to why the first victim had been found naked. It was the oddest thing. Why not let the clothes go up in smoke with the man himself? Now that she knew that Artie had killed the man, it made much more sense that the clothes were removed; not to cover up the identity of the victim but to reveal something about him. And what was there to reveal about Jack Parsons?

Of course, she thought. *If*, as Lady Hansen had told her, Piffers bought expensive clothes for his lover, would Parsons have worn those clothes to come to St Nesbans? He wasn't, after all, expecting to see his lover here. Lord and Lady Hansen should have already been in Florence; that was their original plan, but Parsons would have wanted to dress in his best clothes.

Suddenly, it all made sense. Artie had removed the clothing to gain an advantage over Piffers. Piffers had killed Artie in a fit of pique for daring to threaten him. Now, all she had to do was to find the clothes. Strolling as she had done without a great deal of thought to her path, Lady Gayle realised that she had arrived at the place where the shooting had taken place on the first day. She'd passed by here before looking for a good hiding place, but what if Artie had wanted it to be somewhere where the clothes could be found more easily? Although he must have known he'd be hung for the murder of Jack Parsons, the clothes would implicate Lord Hansen, and he would be convicted too.

Gaspod woofed to attract her attention. She called to him, but he ignored her as he pawed at the entrance to a badger sett. 'Leave that, boy. You don't want to upset old Brock,' she said, using the old countryman's term for badgers.

Gaspod kept pawing at the hole, and she came over to see what he was up to. The dog dug excitedly, and she tried to pull him away until she saw what he had in his mouth—a stiff collar which was missing its studs. 'Good boy,' she said, and the dog dug harder. A tie followed the collar, and then a waistcoat. Before long, she had an entire gentleman's outfit, complete with its Saville Row tailor's label.

She patted Gaspod on the head, knowing that it would

not take the inspector long to track down the tailor and then the customer who had paid for the clothes. Folding the clothes into a neat pile, she bent to pick them up but dropped them when she heard the click as a shotgun was loaded and snapped shut.

CHAPTER TWENTY-SEVEN

'I WOULDN'T DO THAT IF I WERE YOU, LADY GAYLE.' THE VOICE was soft and low but dripping with menace.

Lady Gayle turned around to see Lord Hansen pointing a twelve-bore shotgun at her. 'Oh heck,' she murmured. 'Where on earth did he get that from?'

'You really should have drunk the brandy,' said Lord Hansen, with a smile playing around his lips. His eyes, on the other hand, were cold, with no amusement lurking there. 'I do hate interfering women. Why couldn't you have drunk the cyanide and left well alone?'

'Not my nature, Piffers,' she replied with a jaunty air she wasn't feeling. She pushed the dog behind her. Although, if Piffers shot her, she was sure he'd have no qualms about shooting poor Gaspod. 'I like to know the truth. For instance, why did you have to kill Jack Parsons? He wasn't here to blackmail you, was he? He was simply here to see Binky about the debts with William Saffron.'

'Saffron?' said Piffers, shaking his head. 'Where in the deuces does he come into it?'

'He's a gangster from London. He bought the IOUs that the Pope sold.'

Lord Hansen barked a laugh. 'You don't have a clue, do you,' he said. 'The Pope didn't sell the IOUs, she simply used Saffron to provide her with enforcers. She got fed up with people like dear old Binky skipping out on their debts. It's not as if she could do the strong-arm stuff herself. Not with her being a lady. Or at least trying to pretend she's a lady.'

Lady Gayle frowned. 'I thought the Pope was a man,' she said weakly.

Lord Hansen pursed his lips, shaking his head emphatically. 'Nope, sorry,' he said. 'It's a rather ironic name really.'

Lady Gayle groaned as the gears in her brain finally clunked, and the ideas fell into place. Of course, Mrs Bishop. She was the lady who wasn't a lady. 'I've been trying to work out why she was here.' She rubbed her forehead with the back of her hand.

'Too bad you won't be telling anyone,' replied Lord Hansen. He pulled the hammers back and raised the gun to nestle the stock in the crook of his shoulder.

As he lowered his cheek against the lock, Lady Gayle pursed her lips. How I do hate guns, she thought. She glanced at the clothes on the ground by her feet, wondering if she could throw something at his lordship to distract him. *A shoe, perhaps?* Gaspod whimpered and nuzzled her hand with his cold nose. *No, it's too risky, and even if I were able to distract him, what then? I'm not going to be able to wrestle the gun from him, am I?*

Furious at the realisation that the inspector could have been right after all, Lady Gayle cursed her weakness. She closed her eyes, waiting for the explosion and the pain that she was sure would follow. When the shotgun blasted, she covered her ears with her hands and dropped to the ground. Gaspod licked her face, and as she tried to push him away, she was faintly aware that she felt no pain. This wasn't quite how she'd envisaged heaven. Or perhaps she was in the other place? Did they allow dogs in the other place?

'Gigi, are you alright?'

That's odd, she thought. *That sounds like Charles. Why is he here?*

'Can you get up? I don't think you've been shot this time.'

She opened one eye and then the other. Charles was bent over her, concern etched over his face once again, but this time, he was also biting back a smile.

'Get up,' he said. 'I think you've ruined your dress, but you're all in one piece.'

She accepted his hand, and he pulled her upright. A police constable was standing over Lord Hansen with a shotgun in his hand. He leaned down to pick up Lord Hansen's shotgun, broke the weapon open and hooked it over his arm. He gave Lady Gayle a quick nod, as the realisation the man had just saved her life, dawned upon her. She stared open-mouthed at Charles Vickery. 'Why are you always around when I get shot at,' she said.

'Luck,' he said, offering her his arm. 'Shall we?'

As Lady Gayle allowed herself to be walked away from the scene, she sneaked a final look over her shoulder. One police constable was closing the eyes of the recently deceased Lord Hansen, and the other was picking up the pile of clothes she had folded and placing them in a paper bag.

Inspector Coward raised his right hand in greeting, but before she could respond, Charles gripped her elbow and ushered her back to the house.

'Why the hurry, Charles,' said Lady Gayle. 'I would prefer to walk rather than scurry along like a criminal.'

'You've had a shock,' replied Charles. 'Sweet tea is good for shock. Or perhaps a brandy.'

Lady Gayle stopped and wrenched her elbow out of his hands. 'Not brandy,' she said with a wry smile. 'I think I've given up on brandy for the time being.'

'I'm not surprised,' said Charles. 'But some tea, I'll even be your taster if you don't trust anyone.' He gave her a broad grin, but Lady Gayle felt unable to respond.

'So many secrets,' she said. 'Everyone was hiding so many dark secrets.' She turned towards the house, and Gaspod followed close behind. Kicking the leaves which had fallen overnight, she thought about everyone in the house and the secrets they had kept hidden. Even she was not immune from the pandemic.

'Do you have any secrets, Charles,' she mused as they reached the house, although she already had a very good idea of the answer.

He opened the door for her, and she crossed the threshold, feeling the heat hit her. She shuddered.

'Come along,' said Charles, 'you're frozen. I'll get Snelling to bring us some tea. We'll soon have you warmed up.'

Lady Gayle allowed herself to be dragged down the corridor to the drawing room. Charles rang the bell. Snelling took the order for tea and removed Gaspod from the furniture.

'You didn't answer my question, Charles,' said Lady Gayle. 'What are your secrets?'

Charles laughed and moved towards the mantelpiece. He took a cigarette from the case and picked up a lighter. It took him some time to finish his machinations.

Thinking time? Lady Gayle wondered, staring at his back.

'I don't have any secrets,' he said at last, blowing smoke towards the ceiling. 'Pure as the driven snow, that's me.' He ran his thumb across the base of one nostril and gave her a winning smile.

Lady Gayle was not convinced. She already had some inkling of his activities in Atlantic City, thanks to Binky. Granted, she was relieved that he wasn't loaning money to gamblers, although she was perturbed that he appeared to be making a good living from playing poker. *Is he hiding something else?* If he is, she thought, I am determined to uncover what it is.

'I'M GOING to find out how Pamela is,' said Lady Gayle, replacing her teacup on a low table. 'I'll take Gaspod up with me.' With the large hound at her heels, she trotted up the stairs to her room. She knocked and entered, but only Alice was present.

'What's happened?' she asked.

'The doctor and her maid have rushed Lady Collins to hospital,' said Alice.

'Was the emetic any use?' asked Lady Gayle.

Alice shook her head. 'I don't think so. The inspector gave orders for the brandy to be tested. He thought that it must have been a very strong poison.'

Lady Gayle sat on the ottoman at the foot of her bed. 'Lord Hansen is dead. A police constable shot him. He was about to shoot me and Gaspod.'

The dog, on hearing his name, edged closer and placed his jowls on her knee. Lady Gayle fondled his ears.

'I never suspected him as he had an alibi,' Alice replied.

'He did. He had a very good alibi since he got Artie to kill Jack Parsons. Then he killed Artie, and before he was about to kill me, he admitted putting cyanide in the brandy I had here.'

'I think I'd like to go home before too long, milady,' said Alice. 'Just as soon as her young ladyship is home from the hospital and settled.'

'Yes, good idea,' said Lady Gayle. 'Me too.'

CHAPTER TWENTY-EIGHT

When Lady Gayle returned to the drawing room to see Charles, Snelling had brought fresh tea and hot toddies. Lady Gayle sat alone with Charles while they waited for news about Lady Collins.

She poured them both some tea and rested her head against the back of the sofa. It had been an exhausting few days, with very little chance of the rest and relaxation she'd hoped for.

'I owe you an apology, Charles,' said Lady Gayle. 'I thought you were the Pope.'

Charles laughed. 'No, not me,' he said. 'Although my friendship with Mrs Bishop has spanned a few years now. I knew her husband during the war.'

Lady Gayle sipped her tea and waited.

'He was a munitions manufacturer, as I said before,' Charles began. 'After the war, we had the idea of making some money in the new world.'

'Did he go to Atlantic City with you?'

Charles shook his head. 'No, he simply provided the

investment. I was in the thick of it, but he did get me out before I was arrested.'

'I did hear you left in rather a hurry.'

Charles grinned. 'I did that,' he said. 'The Pinkertons were on to me. They did not approve of my breaking prohibition, and I had to decamp with some speed. John Bishop helped expedite my escape. But by the time I made it back home, he was dead. From a heart attack, or so I'm told. That's when I met with Rose Bishop. It was just business with us, Gigi, never anything more than that.'

'Yes, Charles. I know, but you don't owe me an explanation. Lady Sylvia, perhaps, but not me.'

'What has Bundle said?'

'She thought you were after Sylvia's money.' Lady Gayle twisted her teacup in its saucer.

'She's a very astute woman. Although I would have preferred someone with more wit and sparkle, I do believe I could have made Sylvia happy... Eventually.'

Lady Gayle nodded. She ignored the remark about someone with more wit, focussing instead on the thought that Charles would have made Sylvia happy. She was surprised to discover that she believed him. Realising she'd reached a decision, she placed the teacup on the table. 'I'm going to wait until Bundle and baby Sylvia are back in residence, and then I will head back to Bethencourt Castle,' she said, thinking of the new comforts of a centrally heated home.

'That sounds like a very good plan,' said Charles.

'What are you going to do?'

'I think I'm going to stay at my club for a while. I have some clients I need to see.'

'You've never said that you were still in business, Charles,' said Lady Gayle.

'I continue to dabble,' replied Charles. 'I don't have a job as such. Pater still provides me with a small allowance. When he sees fit...'

'I see,' said Lady Gayle. 'I fear I do have a job now, and I must return to it soon.' She raised her cup to her lips, frowned and sniffed at it before taking a sip.

'Perhaps you'll feel safer when you're at home again,' suggested Charles.

Lady Gayle gave him a quick smile. 'Safer?' she said. 'That's such a nice idea, isn't it?'

They sat in silence for a while longer. Neither felt the need to fill the quiet with conversation.

The door opened, and Lady Hansen entered, followed by Sir William Greenwood.

'Would you like tea?' offered Lady Gayle. 'I seem to have taken on the role of hostess whilst Bundle is laid up.'

'That would be lovely,' said Lady Hansen whilst at the same time Sir William said he'd prefer something stronger.

Lady Gayle poured tea, and Charles rose to pour a whisky for Sir William. All four gathered around the fire, and the silence resumed.

'We've made a decision,' said Lady Hansen after a few moments. 'Willie and I are going to Florence after all. Willie has changed our travel arrangements. I put in a trunk call to the hotel, and they can host us from next week.'

'When do you leave?' said Lady Gayle. She glanced at them both sitting so closely together, gazing into each other's eyes. They looked incredibly happy, and for a moment, she experienced a slight flicker of envy.

'Tomorrow,' said Lady Hansen. 'I don't see any point in delaying any longer. We should have left before New Year in any case.'

Lady Gayle nodded. 'I wish you a pleasant trip,' she said.

'What about your husband, my lady?' said Charles.

Lady Hansen glowered at him. 'There will be a quiet funeral,' she said. 'He was the last of his line, and I don't suppose many of his friends will want to attend the funeral of a murderer, do you, Lord Charles?'

'I rather imagine not,' replied Charles. Lady Gayle glanced at him, but he reclined in his chair, eyes closed. She imagined that he was thinking about his friend.

UNABLE TO BEAR the chilly atmosphere any longer, Lady Gayle rose and strolled into the hallway.

'Snelling,' she said on seeing the butler hovering nearby. 'Would you mind telephoning Bethencourt Castle and letting Mr Fredericks know that I'll be returning home by the weekend?'

'Very good, my lady,' came the reply.

Lady Gayle trudged upstairs to the blue room as she was overcome by fatigue. Alice was already in the process of packing clothes that had been worn and required laundering.

'You may as well pack everything, Alice,' said Lady Gayle. 'I think it's time to go home.'

Alice gave her a soft smile. 'Would you like to rest, milady?' she said.

Lady Gayle looked at Gaspod, who sat expectantly on the hearth rug. 'I would,' she said, 'but I don't think Gaspod would ever forgive me. I'll take a turn around the gardens, but I will rest before dinner.'

. . .

THE FOLLOWING MORNING, Lady Gayle asked for the little Austin to be brought around after breakfast. Once again dressed warmly, she set off for the cottage hospital.

Lady Pamela Collins was in a side room and was not the only occupant. She looked at her new visitor and glanced at Mrs Bishop, who had been reading to her from a broadsheet.

Mrs Bishop laid her newspaper on the edge of the bed. She gave Lady Gayle a confused look. 'Haven't you done enough?' she said. 'Lady Collins needs her rest, especially in her condition.'

Lady Gayle's hands flew to her mouth. 'I only came to say how sorry I am,' was all she could utter.

'My baby is fine,' snapped Lady Collins, 'but I will have to bring him up all on my own now. Artie would have made a fantastic father.'

'I'm sorry,' Lady Gayle repeated, unsure of what else to say. It was on the tip of her tongue to mention that Lord Collins would have been hung as a murderer, and therefore, raising the child alone was something of a moot point. 'Lord Hansen is dead.' There didn't seem to be anything else she could say.

'Then he got away easily, didn't he?' said Mrs Bishop. 'Lord Hansen should have hung. Spent night after night in prison knowing that the hangman was coming for him.'

Lady Gayle shivered. 'I thought knowing he couldn't harm anyone ever again would help,' she said. 'I'm sorry I came.'

'So am I,' replied Lady Collins. 'I will be returning to Scotland and my husband's estate at the weekend, Lady Gayle. I doubt we'll see each other again. Good day to you.' She shook out the newspaper and returned her attention to the stories within.

Mrs Bishop rose, leaned over to give Lady Collins a kiss on the cheek and indicated that Lady Gayle should leave the room.

Well really, thought Lady Gayle. However, since there was nothing more to be said, she simply turned around and left.

Mrs Bishop was hard on her heels. 'Don't be too angry with her,' she said, pulling the door closed. 'Not all of us are cut out to be widows. I manage rather well on my own. Much better than I had anticipated. You do, too, I see. Lady Collins will remarry in time. She needs a man in her life.'

Lady Gayle stared at the other woman but found it hard to disagree. Although they would never be kindred spirits, they had reached an understanding of sorts. She held out her hand, and Mrs Bishop shook it.

'Goodbye, my dear,' she said.

CHAPTER TWENTY-NINE

Baby Sylvia was just on the point of waking when Lady Gayle walked into the nursery. Bundle was sitting in a rocking chair, ready to nurse her daughter. It was a decision that her ladyship had had to force through, as many people, including her own mother, said she should employ a wet nurse. Bundle had her own ideas, and in any case, she'd been told that it was a good way to lose all the baby weight.

The sight of mother and daughter together as the baby drank was almost more than Lady Gayle could bear. But she suddenly understood why the image of Madonna and child was used so often in paintings. It felt like a privilege to be there, taking part in such an intimate moment.

She cocked her head towards Mary, who had materialised at her side. 'The inspector is getting ready to leave, my lady.' Mary whispered in her ear. 'With his compliments, he told me he would like to say goodbye to you before he goes.'

Lady Gayle nodded and turned towards the door. She did not want to leave the room despite the painful memories and deeply buried emotions that the scene before her brought out.

She blew a kiss at Bundle and baby and made her way to the library.

'You wanted to see me, Inspector?' she said as she entered the room. He was perusing the bookshelves much as he had been when she first met him in her own library at Bethencourt Castle.

He turned to face her slowly as if he could not pull himself away from the books. 'Are you a keen reader?' she asked, finding to her surprise that she was interested in the answer.

'Sometimes,' he said. 'Won't you sit down?' He sat on one of the sofas close to the fire.

Lady Gayle sat opposite him, giving him a small smile.

'Mother and baby are well?' asked the inspector.

'Yes, very well,' replied Lady Gayle. What does he want? she thought, wondering if he was trying to lull her into a false sense of security. *He's definitely up to something.* 'Was there something in particular you wanted, Inspector?'

'You put yourself in danger again,' he said.

'I didn't do it on purpose. I went for a walk, and Lord Hansen came upon me. It wasn't my fault.'

'I worry about you.' Inspector Coward gazed into the flames, the glow from the fire giving his face a flushed appearance. He turned to face her, and she realised that the flush wasn't from the fire at all. 'I don't expect you to return my feelings, but—'

'Please, Inspector, let me stop you there. I—'

'Oh, I know you have feelings for Lord Charles,' said Inspector Coward.

Lady Gayle lost control of her jaw as her mouth fell open.

She snapped it shut immediately. 'I have no idea where you got that notion,' she said. 'Charles and I are friends, old friends granted, but nothing more than that. However, in any case—'

She stopped speaking at the sound of the library door opening. Binky strolled in, followed by Mrs Bishop and a small bespectacled man with a clipboard.

'I'm sorry, Gigi,' said Binky. 'Mrs B and I are just having a chat about things. You know.'

'I do, Binky darling,' she said, grateful for the opportunity to escape the all too embarrassing conversation. 'I'm just going back to the nursery to have a last cuddle with your daughter.'

'Splendid idea,' said Binky. 'Why don't you go and see her too, Inspector? She is rather sweet, even if I do say so myself.'

'I will do that, my lord,' said Inspector Coward. 'Thank you.'

He followed Lady Gayle out of the library and up to the nursery. Once again, Lady Gayle was reminded of their first meeting. Were they going to replicate every aspect of that day once more today?

Little Lady Sylvia had finished her meal when they entered the nursery and was being wrapped in a white knitted shawl by the nursemaid. The delicate filigree pattern spread out in spirals from a central circle, forming an intricate maze. As the nursemaid placed the baby in Lady Gayle's arms, the shawl seemed to float with the movement; the smell of summer flowers and lavender, which permeated its folds, was released and filled her nostrils.

Lady Gayle closed her eyes for a moment. *If I simply focus on the shawl, I don't have to think about the baby.*

'My lady.' The inspector's soft voice was close by her ear. Lady Gayle opened her eyes to discover that he was standing next to her, his grey eyes intent on those of the baby. 'Beautiful,' he said.

Lady Gayle plonked the baby in his arms and rushed to the nursery window.

'Gigi, are you all right?' asked Bundle. 'You can give the baby to nurse, Inspector.' Coming to stand by her friend at the window, Bundle placed her cool hand on Lady Gayle's shoulder.

'Don't worry about me,' said Lady Gayle. 'It's of no consequence.'

'No consequence? Don't be silly, I can see that it's eating you up. I'd like you to be her godmother, but if you can't bear to hold her, then I wouldn't ask it of you.'

Lady Gayle turned away from the window and hugged Bundle. 'I'd like that,' she said. 'I'd like that very much.' She faced the inspector where he sat cuddling the tiny baby; the nurse hovered anxiously beside him, holding her hands out as if she anticipated having to catch the child at any moment. He was cooing at the infant, and she was watching him with wide eyes. Something stirred deep within Lady Gayle as her heart squeezed. Where on earth was the no-nonsense policeman?

He smiled at her and gave the baby up to her nurse, who looked relieved when her charge was safe and sound in her arms.

'Perhaps we should talk,' he said.

Lady Gayle glanced at Bundle, who gave her an encouraging smile. She nodded, and she and the inspector left the sweet-smelling room. Leading the way downstairs, Lady

Gayle decided the orangery was as good a place as any. With the inspector following her closely, she imagined she felt his breath on her neck. With head hanging, she knew this was a conversation she wanted to avoid at any cost.

When the door was closed, and she was sure that no one would overhear them, Lady Gayle began, but the inspector interrupted.

'I'm sorry,' he said. 'I didn't know.'

'Not many people do,' said Lady Gayle, 'that's rather the point with secrets. No one else is supposed to know them.'

Inspector Coward chuckled, but there was no mirth in the sound. 'And my job is to uncover everyone's secrets. I didn't realise yours was so painful. May I ask what happened?'

'Do you have to?' asked Lady Gayle. She snapped a flower off its stem, staring at the blossom in her hands. *Oh my word, it's already wilting. Perhaps death is all I can bring?* She shook her head and allowed the flower to fall from her hand. *Stuff and nonsense.* Her mother's voice resounded in her head as clearly as if the dowager countess were in the room with them.

'I lost a baby when my husband was killed.' There, she'd said it. It was out in the open, and no harm done. But she knew that she wasn't convincing anyone, least of all herself.

'I don't know if I can have more babies,' she said, 'but what I do know is that I have no intention of putting myself in a situation where I find out. That's the bargain I've made with myself.'

'I am so very sorry,' said Inspector Coward.

'We all have wounds we don't advertise, don't we, Inspector?' she said, referring to his ongoing battle with shellshock. 'We simply carry on the best we can.'

He bowed his head. 'We do,' he said, holding out his hand. 'I understand perfectly. Goodbye, Lady Gayle.'

She took his hand and gave it a firm shake. 'Goodbye, Inspector,' she said, and she turned and walked out of the orangery.

CHAPTER THIRTY

As the small Austin turned into the driveway leading to Bethencourt Castle, Lady Gayle put aside her thoughts of Charles Vickery and Inspector Coward—two very different men with very different qualities to recommend them. Neither of them, however, was Hugh Sexton. Feeling the tears starting to gather, she drew to a halt and concentrated on the vista of her home. True, the responsibility of the estate weighed upon her greatly, but it was no more than it had weighed upon any of the owners before her.

'Milady?' whispered Alice, 'Are you quite well?'

'Yes, Alice. Just happy to be home,' she said.

When they reached the entrance of Bethencourt, Fredericks and a footman were waiting to greet them. The footman helped Alice remove the luggage and carry it into the castle. For once, Fredericks allowed proprieties to be overcome, and Alice walked in the front door loaded down with cases.

Lady Gayle strolled in after her, and once divested of her winter coat, boots, and thick socks, she wandered towards one of the new cast iron radiators. She placed a hand upon it. Then she frowned at her butler.

'I can explain, my lady,' said Fredericks.

'I can hardly wait, Fredericks,' said Lady Gayle. 'Is there a fire in the drawing room? If so, bring me tea there. Alice, could you bring me a shawl down as soon as you get a moment?'

Both servants nodded; one with a bow, the other with a curtsy. Lady Gayle strode to the drawing room and was relieved to see a fire roaring in the grate. Gaspod followed and threw himself into an exhausted heap before the fire.

'It's alright for you,' said Lady Gayle. 'At least you have a fur coat.'

The bloodhound gave her a forlorn expression and laid his jowls on his paws, raising his head only briefly when Fredericks returned with the tea tray.

The tray was set down on the low table between the two sofas, which faced each other in front of the fire.

'Shall I pour, my lady?' said Fredericks.

'I think *I'll* pour,' said Lady Gayle. '*You* can tell me what's been happening while I've been away. Presumably, there's been a problem with the plumber?'

'Oh, my lady,' replied Fredericks. 'I scarcely know where to begin.'

'The beginning is usually the best place, I find, Fredericks.' Lady Gayle waved her hand at the sofa opposite, and with some hesitation, Fredericks finally perched himself on the edge of the seat.

'As you can see, my lady, the radiators have been installed but not without considerable noise and upset.

'Mrs Mitchell had a terrible time keeping the maids in order. Mr Jenkins, the plumber, made very lewd remarks to the girls. Quite upset they were. I had words with him, of course. So did Mrs Mitchell, but it made no difference. There were tears below stairs every day.'

'What kind of lewd remarks?' said Lady Gayle.

Fredericks looked stricken. 'I don't know that I could repeat them, my lady.'

'I see. Please continue,' said Lady Gayle.

'We left it so that the maids would clear up after he'd left for the day. And he did like to leave quite early in the afternoon.'

'That doesn't seem like a very long day,' said Lady Gayle. 'Did he take a lunch break?'

'Oh yes, my lady,' replied Fredericks. 'He drove to the village every day at noon and took his luncheon in the Bethencourt Arms.

'As my lady might imagine, he was not very industrious in the afternoons.'

'One might indeed,' replied Lady Gayle. 'Tell me, who recommended this paragon to us? I thought my father had put everything in place before he died.'

'He did, my lady,' replied Fredericks. 'I believe that Colonel Gosforth recommended the man to your father. I have taken the liberty of asking in the village, and whilst the man may have been very industrious at one time, he has gradually become worse over the last few years. He's not taken well to civilian life after the war, my lady.'

'But the war has been over for four years, Fredericks. Surely he's not still using that as an excuse?'

'I am given to understand, my lady, that things have gone more and more downhill over the last four years. He had a good reputation before the war, but since then, his reputation has suffered. A suffering, it would appear, all of his own making.'

'As you say, Fredericks. Well, I think all we can do is find another plumber who can pick up where this chap has left off. Can I leave that with you?'

Lady Gayle turned her head as Alice walked into the room carrying a shawl. 'Milady,' she began. 'There's a problem with your jewellery box.'

'What kind of a problem, Alice?'

'It's gone, milady. I placed it in the safe in your study, and it's not there.'

'Oh, dash it all. Fredericks, what do you know about this?'

'I cannot explain it, my lady. Mr Jenkins wasn't allowed to go into the study unaccompanied. When he installed the radiator, Owens was with him all the time.'

'Perhaps not all the time, Fredericks. Could you call Owens for me, please? Alice, we'd better take a look at this safe.'

Lady Gayle pushed herself from the sofa, taking in and releasing a deep breath. All joy at returning home had dissipated. Alice opened the door to the study for her.

The oil painting which normally hid the safe was on the floor leaning against the wall, and the safe door hung open, presumably as Alice had left it after her discovery. Lady Gayle crossed the room in a few short strides.

'What on earth?' She opened and closed the door, checking the damage on both sides. Inside the safe were little spirals of metal. The floor beneath it bore the signs of being recently swept. 'It's been drilled open. Alice, we need to call the police.'

As Alice dashed from the room, Lady Gayle studied the contents of the safe more closely. No papers had been touched as far as she could see. All that was missing were some items of jewellery, none of which were very valuable, but they had been placed in the safe for safekeeping. She chuckled at the phrase, however, keeping the items under lock and key tended to deter all but the most determined thieves. This thief, it appeared, had been very determined. Why? She flopped into the chair behind the recently inherited desk and played with the drawers. Noticing that they were not fully closed as they should have been, she pulled out the large bottom drawer. Wrapped in newspaper at the bottom of the space were the items they all sought.

She turned at the sound of someone entering the room. 'The police are on their way, my lady,' said Fredericks.

Lady Gayle nodded. 'And Owens?' she said, placing the wrapped items on the desk.

Fredericks, unable to help himself, raised both eyebrows. 'He will be here directly, my lady.'

'Thank you. You said Colonel Gosforth recommended the man to my father? Do we know if the Colonel has used Mr Jenkins' services since the war?'

'I can enquire my lady.'

'Please do. Ah, Owens, do come in. I want to talk to you about the plumber, Mr Jenkins.'

Sadly, Owens was unable to add anything to the information Lady Gayle had gleaned for herself. He denied leaving the plumber alone for any length of time. 'Mr Fredericks asked me to keep an eye on him, and that's what I did, my lady.'

'He was never left alone in this room?' said Lady Gayle. She regarded her father's valet with a cool gaze, noticing the way he was unable to meet her eyes. 'Owens?'

'I had a bad stomach, my lady. I kept needing to visit the... well, you know.'

Lady Gayle inclined her head. 'Thank you, Owens,' she said. 'That will be all.'

As the poor valet scurried from the room, she turned

her attention back to the safe. If done quietly enough, it would have been easy for the plumber to drill the lock while the valet was otherwise engaged. However, since the jewels had been hidden virtually in plain sight, there must have been some trickery at play.

She had a very good idea of who was responsible for the subterfuge.

CHAPTER THIRTY-ONE

Deciding that she needed some fresh air, Lady Gayle made her way to her bedroom, changed into riding breeches, and then strode to the stables for the grey horse that was now hers to ride.

When she entered the stable yard, the head groom, Shepherd, was brushing Plantagenet down.

'Shall I saddle him for you, my lady?' he said.

'Just bring me the tack,' she replied. 'I can do it. Oh, and Shepherd, the new saddle that my mother bought me for Christmas.'

'My lady,' replied Shepherd. He returned promptly with the brand-new saddle that would enable her to sit astride the horse. She was still surprised that her mother had given her such a gift, but it spoke so much about the dowager countess' transition into the principles of the new century. Perhaps the future was brighter than it had looked only a few short weeks ago?

She mounted the eighteen-hand high grey using the mounting block and gathered him into a smart trot, and they clip-clopped out the yard. Choosing to avoid bridleways that had caused much upset on recent rides, Lady Gayle set off towards the river and the plot of land that Colonel Gosforth wanted to claim as his own. For Lady Gayle, it was a treasured spot where she had spent happy times as a child, fishing with her Great Uncle, her father, her cousins, and her beloved brother.

She sighed. All of them were gone now. The younger men had not survived the Great War, and the older men had not survived the aftermath. Placing the reins in her left hand, Lady Gayle scratched Plantagenet on his withers. The horse shuddered and shook himself. Lady Gayle knew it was his tickly spot, and she patted him on the side of his neck. He bobbed his head up and down in reply.

Drawing nearer the river, she spied a rounded figure on the bank. She pressed her heels to the horse's side, and they increased speed. As horse and rider grew close, the figure turned and ran for the boundary fence, waddling as fast as he could move.

Lady Gayle halted the horse and pursed her lips. 'Very well, Colonel Gosforth,' she muttered, 'you can run for now, but you cannot hide, and we will talk soon.'

She wheeled the horse around and headed out to inspect the far reaches of her estate.

The End

Please flip the page for a note on spellings used by this British author.

To my lovely readers,

A very long time ago, I was born in Britain. I love this little island and all its quirks. There are some things that I don't love, but they will never be in the Cassie Rush books.

I do use UK English spellings, punctuation, and grammar, including the "u" in colour, humour, rigour, and other words I can't think of right now. I also use an "s" where Americans tend to prefer a "z", such as cosy/cozy. In fact, my laptop just auto-corrected cozy!

I read a vast number of cosy mysteries written by American writers. I love the sarcasm, humour and I especially love the paranormal, witchy novels. It's also made me acutely aware of how the grammar differs between the two languages. It still jars when I read something like, "The dress fit perfectly" instead of, what to me is the correct form, "The dress fit**ted** perfectly", but I know it's different, not wrong.

I hope you'll forgive me for sticking with the language I've been using all my life.

Thanks,
Cassie
Suffolk, UK
April 2023

REVIEWS

I do hope you enjoyed this encounter with Lady Gayle Summer, Countess Bethencourt.

If so I wonder if you would be so kind as to leave me a review on Amazon or Goodreads?

For paperback readers, please look out for the review request email.

Please join my newsletter here, if you would like to keep in touch, and hear news about my upcoming books and latest releases

Thank you,
Cassie

Acknowledgments

Getting a book ready for publication is a huge team effort and I'm lucky to be surrounded by such supportive friends and dedicated professionals to make my books the best they can be.

Huge thanks to my friend Heidi Robertson who did yet another read through for me after my lovely editor Sheryl Marshall had run her blue pencil over it.

To the fabulous Molly Burton who creates the magnificent covers for the Lady Gayle Summer series, the Eastwold-by-the-Sea series and for the Kim David series that will be out very soon.

Finally, a thanks to the launch team, who read through and helped catch the Hide-and-Seek universal champions – the typo. If you find any, let me know. I hate them as much as you do.

Thanks, Cassie
Suffolk 2023

ALSO BY CASSIE RUSH

EASTWOLD BY THE SEA SERIES

Raising the Roof

Literary Murder

On the Stroke of Death

My BookA Slice of Murder

LADY GAYLE SUMMER SERIES

Summers Slain

Summer Knights

Summer Secrets

Coming soon — Summer Races. The flat racing season has begun, and Lord Ridgewell has bought himself a racehorse. What could possibly go wrong?

About the Author

Hi there, my name is Cassie Rush and I'm a British author of cosy mysteries set in the English country- or seaside.

I absolutely love the coastal town of Southwold which is a short drive up the coast from where I live. It's why I chose to set my popular, *Eastwold by the Sea* series there. Although my version of the town is entirely fictional as I like to move streets around. I hate it when an author sets a story somewhere you know well and gets details wrong, don't you?

I have been a fan of Agatha Christie all my life and I adore the other golden age authors. I especially enjoy the stories of Miss Marple, Father Brown, Brother Cadfael and Lord Peter Wimsey.

I was really lucky at school (let's not talk about how long ago that was though) to have brilliant and enthusiastic history teachers. It's given me a lifelong love of history and all the tales that the past has to offer.

I also write as Caroline Goldsworthy—these books are rather darker with more graphic content.